BIGASS SQUIRRELS
by Patrick MacAdoo

Bigass Squirrels

ISBN - 978-0-9909656-3-3

Printed in the United States of America

Chapter One

Skkkrreeeeekkkk.

Larry jerked awake and wrenched the steering wheel away from the metallic screech outside his door. He righted the Olds, the violent skew causing a momentary warp in the churning muddle of Black Sabbath's *Trashed* before the tape deck's spindles resumed correct speed.

Darkness smeared beyond the reach of the Olds' high-beams. Larry squinted. The whorls and tassels of cornstalks frayed the underside of the night sky all the way to the horizon. Gravel pinged against the Delta 88's undercarriage, the knocks reverberating through the soles of his ratty sneakers.

Larry whispered, "Where the hell am I?"

The tang of whiskey irritated his nostrils. An open bottle of Jack nestled against his crotch. Strawberry Hill empties rolled and clinked against one another on the backseat's floorboard. He muddled backwards for some mental landmark, but the days and nights blurred until he plunged into the mechanical fugue of the cramped flight to New York, the antiseptic scent of the examining room, the talk show host's craggly, tanned face, silver hair, and blinding teeth as he announced the results of the paternity test, Deanne bawling her eyes out while fleeing backstage, Kirk vowing in front of both the cameras and the studio audience that he would step up and be a good daddy to little Bobby …

Larry scrunched his eyelids shut. He tried to banish the whole mess but it was too huge. So huge that he'd gone straight to the airport's parking lot and drove the Olds to the nearest liquor store, then south, away from Madison, away from home. By now it must be all over town how he'd worked two jobs to provide for a woman who'd lied about the baby being his.

"MOTHERFUCKER!"

Larry's eyelids snapped open. Lights flared in his rearview mirror. He groaned. Dudes piled into the bed of a tricked-out pickup. The truck whipped a U-turn in the gravel and skidded after him, its souped-up engine roaring over the steady thrum of Black Sabbath. He gunned the Olds. His clammy palms slipped on the wheel. They knew the roads. They'd run him into the ditch and give him a righteous ass-kicking.

He barked a harsh laugh. He took a slug of Jack and cranked up the tunes as the mix tape transitioned to Iron Maiden's *Die With Your Boots On*. The muscle truck gained on him. Over the redlining engines and the heavy-metal throb, the rednecks' whoops and hollers promised skull-bashing and mudhole-stomping.

He gritted his teeth as he guided the Olds into a slow curve. He gritted his teeth harder, resisting the urge to ease up on the gas pedal. He forced himself to ignore the speedometer's needle. He shook, wanting to look, wanting to slow down, all he ever wanted was to be a good dad, all he wanted was for things to go back like they were … he barked another harsh laugh. Now he knew why she wouldn't marry him.

The Olds fishtailed out of the curve. He straightened her out, then took another pull of whiskey. He barely felt the heat tumble down his numbed throat, but his cheeks hadn't stopped burning since New York. Maybe the burn would never go away.

He glanced at the rearview. He'd put a little distance between himself and the rednecks, who obviously hadn't had the balls to take the curve at top speed. He eased a hair up on the gas pedal. The Illinois hills, covered in corn, seemed to stretch to forever. *Forever*.

He took another belt of Jack. His mom and dad, already disappointed that he hadn't gone to college, mortified that he'd shacked up with some girl he'd knocked up at a kegger, they'd exchange the humiliation of being the grandparents of a bastard for that of being the parents of the town joke. Misery would darken his mother's eyes. Fury would harden his dad's. A sudden, chilly silence would fall whenever he entered any room containing only them. They would talk about little else except what they were going to do about him. The guys at the factory would never let him live it down. Neither would the regulars at the bar. By now, probably the whole town knew. No woman would be caught dead with him. Pretty soon, the whole wide world would know. No woman anywhere would ever be caught dead with him. Everything was ruined. Forever.

He chugged the bottle dry and pitched it out the window. He gripped the wheel with both hands. He leaned forward and closed his eyes. The wind whipped his face and howled in his ears. He figured that rolling the Olds in a cornfield probably wouldn't kill him. He needed to find a cement underpass to ram.

He opened his eyes. The pickup surged abreast. A skinhead, his face contorted into a savage leer, leaned his flinty torso out of the passenger's window and flipped Larry off. Two more riders crammed the truck's cab between the screaming skinhead and the driver. A half-dozen rednecks capered in the truck's bed, some brandishing wooden baseball bats with swaying links of chain bolted onto their barrels.

The impression of shattered teeth pulsed in his mouth. He imagined broken bones and squeaky wheelchairs. He flattened the gas pedal. The pickup inched close enough for the skinhead to smack a palm on the Olds' roof. They were gonna run him into the ditch. He saw no mercy in their bloodthirsty faces.

The truck braked. The dudes in the bed held on for dear life, the dudes in the cab whiplashed against the dash. The skinhead almost did a header out the window. Larry spotted the sharp curve out of the corner of his eye. The Olds dipped. He banged his head on the roof. The Olds riffled through cornstalks then jerked to a halt. His chest whomped into the steering wheel.

He gasped for breath. Truck doors slammed. Somebody snarled, "Let's teach this dickless fuck a lesson." They rustled closer through the corn. He couldn't get the door open. Another one yelled, "Hey, c'mon guys, let's get the hell out'a here!" A closer voice said, "I'm gonna rip him a new asshole."

Larry shouldered the door open and flopped onto downed stalks. He levered himself up to his hands and knees, but he collapsed under a wave of dizziness. He curled up and covered his head in anticipation of the first clod-hopper stomp.

Somebody yelled, "Cops!" They crashed through the corn away from him. Gravel spit from under tires. In what seemed like a heartbeat later, strobing red penetrated his eyelids. A radio squawked. Instinct took over and he tried to get up to make a run for it. He rose to his feet, staggered, then toppled, snapping more stalks before thudding into the dirt. He stayed down.

Chapter Two

Two letters into his first name Larry stopped. He scoffed. He'd started writing his first name in the box where his last name was supposed to go. If he asked the bartender for another application he would seem like an idiot. He took a sip of his ice water and waited for the fire in his cheeks to die down. With a couple of deliberate pen strokes he made the capital 'L' into a capital 'D' and the following 'a' into an 'o.' He wrote the rest of his last name and contemplated his work. The thick blue of the first two letters made the rest of his chicken scratch look ridiculous. Realizing he'd have to do the same to his first name in order to make it match, he sighed, then began to thicken the skinny lines.

He scrunched his eyes shut and rubbed his eyelids. He didn't know why he was bothering. The job was a longshot. A couple of other guys, including the dude on his left, were also filling out applications. Larry would bet anything that a stack of resumés from local yokels, with whom the owner of Bub's Pub probably grew up, crowded a desk in the bar's back office.

The fancy-shmancy CD jukebox switched from some lame country ballad to George Thorogood's *One Bourbon, One Scotch, One Beer*. The ode to daytime boozing inspired a couple dudes back by the pool tables to play air guitar on their cues and goosed a few random whoops from the crowd, which was pretty decent for an afternoon. Larry figured that the foxy blonde bartender drew most of the overwhelmingly male population. Even if he lucked out and landed the gig, he doubted that day shifts at this dim saloon would yield the kind of cash he needed to claw his way out of the hole. Deanne had drained their joint accounts and maxed out their credit cards. The Judge, while outlining the expensive terms of the DUI, had scolded Larry about how lucky he was to escape the wreck with only a few cuts and bruises. He'd spent the week in jail because he couldn't afford to bail himself out. He was out on his own recognizance and forbidden from leaving the state. He had less than a hundred bucks in his pocket, and he had no idea how he was gonna pay for the repairs to the Olds. He didn't feel very goddamned lucky.

The applicant on Larry's left raised and waggled his empty bottle of Murray's Finest, a local beer, Larry guessed, and hollered, "Wench, another brew!"

The stocky mug-sipper at Larry's right elbow muttered, "*Asshole*."

The bottle-waggler rotated his face towards Larry, then said, "What'd you say?"

Larry thought his warped reflection in the asshole's mirrored sunglasses looked a little scruffy, but the dude's stringy brown hair and his unruly handlebar mustache made Larry feel better about his own slapdash appearance. The dude's sideburns bushed down to his chin, where two parallel lines of raised white scar tissue slanted across the clean-shaven skin. A blue denim jacket, faded and sleeveless and worn over a sallow tee shirt, along with skintight jeans and black leather wristbands, completed the dude's half-assed attempt to look biker-tough. The dude's shoddy sneakers, skinny arms, and pint-sized frame, which, even though they were seated, Larry estimated at barely over five feet tall, ruined the roughneck affect. A whiff of unwashed armpit wafted over Larry. He suppressed a grimace and said, "I didn't say anything."

The little wannabe hardass held his pose for a second, then returned to his application. Larry eased out a silent breath. The last thing he needed was to tangle with this asshead and end up back in jail. He stole a peek at the third-grader scrawl on the dude's application, then returned to his own work. Between the dude's dropout-style penmanship and his beer drinking while applying, Larry was beginning to suspect that the position at this walk-in closet-sized pub on Murray's town square wasn't particularly prized by the locals. He rolled the pen between his fingers. He needed to start making money, or he'd be forced to crawl back home with his tail tucked between his legs. He re-gripped the Bic and resumed writing.

The bartender placed a fresh bottle on the lacquered wooden bartop. Larry's neighbor took his sweet time fishing a crumpled dollar out of his battered brown wallet. He handed the bill over while huffing, "Took ya long enough."

Larry detected nothing bogus nor flustered in the bartender's pleasant white smile. Her green eyes remained placid. A smattering of light freckles speckled the bridge of her delicate nose. Her jeans clung to her slim thighs and hips, her tight, long-sleeved gray tee shirt accented her flat stomach, which made the swell of her handful-sized boobs all the more unignorable. Larry couldn't locate the raised outline of a bra.

"Can I getcha something?" One brow arched higher than the other over her sparkling eyes.

A deep burn flooded into Larry's cheeks. He shook his head.

She pivoted, her sandy blonde curls bouncing around her shoulders, and she whisked away to the cash register. She returned with the asshole's change, a quarter, which he pocketed as she ranged down the bar for more customers. The asshole muttered, "Twat," loud enough for her to hear but low enough to pretend that she wasn't supposed to.

Her gait didn't show so much as a twitch, but Larry bristled, and the guy on his right balled up his lumpy fists. The impulse to say something shivered through Larry. He closed his eyes. His silence stoked his suspicion that he really was a coward. After all, he was in hiding. He opened his eyes and stared into the bar's back mirror. Maybe he was just taking the easy way out. Maybe he should go back home and face the music.

The bartender glided by and plucked the asshole's empty bottle from the bartop. She halted, then said, "You okay, hon?"

Larry blinked away from his haze. He managed a weak smile. He knew the lilt in her voice was all about getting tips, but that knowledge couldn't kill the slight tingle he felt. He nodded, and opened his mouth, about to tell her he was fine with his ice water.

The asshole said, "I'll be okay after you show me your tits."

Larry winced. "C'mon man."

The guy on Larry's right shoved away from the bar, the undersides of his wooden stool's legs screeching across the tiles, and he shot to his feet while bellowing, "You apologize you little shit!"

Larry found himself standing between the bloody-eyed, slightly weaving brawler and the asshole, who remained seated. The asshole didn't bother to remove his sunglasses. He performed a slow turn of his head and growled through gritted teeth, "Make me."

Larry stepped back, and as the combatants hit the floor, he moved the nearest chairs and table out of the way. The grapplers rolled around and looped ineffectual punches into each other's shoulders and ribs. Larry figured they'd tire themselves out, but then the other patrons crowded in, and began to egg them on and re-energize their flagging efforts. The bartender was hustling toward the bar's cutout, no doubt meaning to intervene. Larry took a deep breath. He reached down and grabbed the brawler's thumb, then bent it back, forcing the brawler to let go and rise from the asshole. Larry lowered himself, using his shins to roll the asshole sideways, then pressed his kneecap into the asshole's back until he pinned the asshole on his belly. He released the brawler's thumb and prepared for retaliation, but much to his relief, the brawler backed away. He captured the asshole's right arm, bent it behind the asshole's back, and yanked it toward his shoulder blades.

The asshole yowled, then screamed, "Lemme up!"

Larry wishboned the asshole's wrist a little higher. "Shut up."

"Get the fuck off'a me!"

Larry cranked up the pressure a little more.

The asshole's voice soared through high registers while he said, "OK OK OK!"

"Here's what's gonna happen. I'm gonna pull you up and I'm gonna walk you out the front door and then I'll letcha go. You got it?"

"Yeah, yeah, yeah!"

Larry ratcheted the strain on the asshole's arm down a bit. He tried to remember the stuff that the security guys back at the night club had taught him. He hauled the asshole to his feet. The sudden motion kicked up a swirl of sour funk from the asshole's greasy clothes. Larry held his breath and exhaled out his nostrils while walking the asshole to the door, which some helpful patron yanked open. Larry squinted and walked the asshole out of the cool dark and into the hot summer sunshine.

Larry gave the asshole a moderate shove while stepping sideways. He kept his hands loose at his hips, ready to raise them into fists if necessary. He slitted his eyes until the bluish tinge decayed from his adjusting vision. The asshole stumbled a few steps before regaining his balance. He spun. He adjusted his askew sunglasses. He flicked strands of stringy brown hair back from his face, and he snarled, "You're gonna be sorry." He started down the sidewalk, his wobbly bearing transforming into a strutting amble, as if he'd just kicked a million asses.

Larry snorted. He reentered the bar.

"Myron," the bartender said, with one hand on her hip and jabbing her index finger at the seated, sheepish brawler, "if you go after Barney Heller I'll have to tell Bub, and you'll be eighty-sixed for a year. Now go out the back and go on home."

Myron, head bowed, got up and shuffled toward the back of the bar. The bartender faced Larry and said, "You still want to work here?"

Larry had to struggle to tamp down a smile at her exasperated face. He nodded.

She bent over his application and wrote something on it, then folded it up and said, "You got my recommendation."

He watched her take his application behind the bar and slip it under the register. Someone behind him said, "Wait till the Heller Boys hear about this."

Chapter Three

Halfway down the porch steps Larry already had the cigarette lit, a move that he now performed with unconscious ease due to Mrs. Reeves' zero-tolerance policy for indoor smoking.

He smirked as the smoke gushed into his lungs. He'd lasted three shifts before the chainsmoking regulars snookered him into taking up the habit again. Deanne had nagged him into quitting in the first place, for the baby's sake. His smirk twisted tight. He'd finally severed all their financial connections, and in the process, he'd learned about how she'd lingered in New York, running up the tab while living it up big time.

He paused at the fork in the cement path and took a long drag off the cigarette. He could stroll around the block or duck over to the side of the house. The cheery blue sky and green foliage of the tree-lined street beckoned to him, but a burst of squeals, the kids down the block squeezing in a little more fun before dinnertime, made him wince. He vowed again that he would never deal drugs to children. He headed for the seclusion between the high hedges and the big white house's side.

He couldn't see another way out of his mess. He'd been damned lucky to land the job at Bub's Pub, but dayshift bartending wasn't gonna cut it, even if what everybody said about the awesome tips during the impending Cheese Days festival was true. He'd discovered over the last two weeks that Murray was a pot-dry town. He had a solid, secure connection, a couple of buddies who'd been moving quantities since high school. As soon as he got his head above water, he'd quit and make a fresh start. All he had to do was avoid the dumb things that got dealers busted, dumb things like dealing to kids, or to shady types who wouldn't think twice about narcing on him to get out of going to jail. He suspected the hardest part would be operating under Mrs. Reeves' scrutiny.

He raised his head as he rounded the corner. He stopped. Two steel cages mashed down the grass next to the narrow cement path. He walked to the nearest cage and puffed his Marlboro.

He'd picked this spot because Mrs. Reeves and her other boarders, whether coming or going or working in the backyard garden, couldn't see him. The tall evergreen hedges blocked the next-door neighbors' view. When he leaned against the house just so, there wasn't a window from which a sneaky housemate could spy on him. He'd never asked permission, but if the cages were a hint to knock it off, and so far Mrs. Reeves hadn't bothered with hints whenever he did anything that bothered her, she wouldn't have left behind the rusty Folgers can that he tossed his stubbed butts in.

He hunkered down in front of one of the knee-high cages. A doorway opened onto a solid gunmetal floor. Just above the floor's center a crusty chunk of apple fritter smeared the end of a thin metal arm that connected to a spring mechanism at the rear of the cage, the mechanism running along the cage's roof and front end, and suspending a sliding door over the cage's entrance.

He scrounged around the hedges until he found a twig with enough length to reach the arm while leaving his hand a safe distance outside the trap. He eased the twig through the little door and poked the metal arm.

Bang!

The door slammed down and snapped the twig in two. He flinched back, tipping over on his butt, his heart whomping against his breastbone. He planted his left palm in the grass in order to brace himself, and with his shaky right hand he brought the half-smoked cigarette to his lips.

Mrs. Reeves scuttled around the house's rear corner. Her thin lips closed over the black hole between her parted dentures and she slowed to a peeved stamp. The wide brim of her straw hat flopped with each stomp of her white canvass sneakers. Her baggy, floral-print shirt, buttoned up to her waddled neck and down to her bony wrists, tucked into her coarse khaki pants that were belted well above the navel, billowed when she halted before him. She wore brown work gloves on her hands, which she curled into fists and planted on her hips. She glared down on him from behind her chunky black wraparound sunglasses. She, standing ramrod straight without a smidge of an old lady hunch, seemed much higher than five foot three.

While he hauled himself up to his feet, she said, "Mister Donaldson! Why are you fooling around with my traps?" With a slow upward tilt of her head she tracked his rise. Her forehead crinkled.

His words tumbled out whiney and high-pitched as he said, "I didn't mean to." He grimaced.

She encroached upon his personal space and he took two steps back. She pivoted, knelt to the grass, and began to reset the trap. "You're darn lucky it didn't chop off your fingers."

"What're they for?"

She pointed at the cigarette smoldering in his right hand. "You'll never find a decent wife if you keep smoking those filthy things."

He was already stooping and stubbing the cigarette against the inside of the coffee can before he could stop himself. He rose into a slouch, shooting for a casual air, and roughened his voice with sarcasm, saying, "Last thing I'm worried about right now is finding a wife."

She stood. One grey eyebrow arced above the rim of her blocky sunglasses. "You don't say?"

He quivered. He'd been dying to spill his guts, but to her, especially the way her ears seemed to perk up? He could imagine her regaling the other churchgoing biddies with his tale of woe. He cleared his throat and inched his heel backwards, preparing for a fast getaway. "What are you trying to trap?" *Besides me, that is.*

Her eyebrow sank under the rim of her sunglasses. Her chin knotted. She hissed, "Squirrels."

"Squirrels?"

"They're a plague!"

Her outburst startled him backwards a half-step. Watching her draw a large breath, a habit that he'd already learned through painful experience always signaled a lecture, he chided himself for egging her on with a question.

"They get into the trash and scatter it all over the street. They gnaw holes in roofs … it cost Esther Bockwinkle thousands to fix her attic after the spring rains! They dig their burrows under the grass, not only ruining lawns, but it's dangerous. Bess Conway broke her ankle in one. She still walks with a limp."

He swiveled a little away from her. He mumbled, "That's terrible."

She bustled past him and examined a barely overgrown stem poking out from the hedges. Her maneuver cut off his retreat. "They spread disease. Mister Reeves, God rest his soul, and I, had a dog,

13

Tuffy, that we had to put down after a squirrel bit him and gave him rabies."

"That's terrible." He calculated that the space between her and the house was too small for him to squeeze through, even if he brushed against the siding.

"They don't just bite dogs, they bite babies too!"

The image of a squirrel springing into a baby carriage was just too much. He couldn't help his derisive pitch, saying, "Really?"

Her thin lips compressed down to a white line. Her face's forward jab made him recoil. "They chew the bark right off fruit trees. It's so bad that nobody in town can have a peach tree or an apple tree, and they rip up gardens, every year the filthy beasts go right for my hybrids, my special herbs nobody else on God's green earth can duplicate, the secret ingredients in my artisan-grade cheese, and two years ago they ruined everything, I had to improvise, and I ended up placing fourth in the Cheese Days *royale fromage* contest, my personal worst showing, all because of those dirty creatures!"

She fumed. The silence seemed to swell and contract. He flailed for something diffusing to say. He hemmed, then said, "What do you do with the squirrels … er, I mean after you trap them?"

Her brow smoothed. Her mouth slitted open. Her brow wrinkled up again and she pointed a gloved index finger at him. "I release them in the park. It's perfectly humane."

He wished she would show some humanity and step out of his way. He'd never seen the cages before. He couldn't see her stuffing the cages into the backseat of her Caddy. He could, however, imagine her hectoring one of her boarders to deal with it. "Seems like waste of time." Her lips slammed together again. He blurted, "I mean it seems like it'd barely make a dent."

"Nothing else I can do. Poison will ruin my herbs. The treehuggers on the town board won't spray the Weeds. They claim it'll get into the groundwater."

"What do weeds have to with it?"

"Not weeds. *The Weeds*." She gestured to the north, toward the tree line bordering her and her neighbors' backyards. "Government property starts at those trees, follows both sides of the creek all the way through town. They say they don't have the funds to keep it nice, so it's horribly overgrown. It's like a jungle back there. Folks call it 'the Weeds.' Darn breeding ground for vermin and pests. River rats, mosquitoes, but especially squirrels."

He craned his neck and gazed at the wall of dark green, which stretched to both horizons as far as he could see. He guessed thousands of squirrels might nest in the Weeds.

"There's an ordinance against firing guns in the town's limits," she said, "or I'd go hunting. Bleeding-heart liberals won't allow it. The Weeds shouldn't count as part of the town. Ought to have a squirrel hunt back there, like they did in my granddaddy's day. Back then, when the squirrels got bad, all the men got together and cleared 'em out in an afternoon. They just got in a big line and walked the town from one end to the other, shot anything with a tail."

He pictured whiskey bottles and shotguns, and bloody carcasses, shredded by excessive firepower. "That would do it."

She bared her gleaming dentures. "These days they don't make 'em like they did in my granddaddy's day. Squirrels are a plague on this town, all because the men around here don't have the guts to do what needs doing."

Chapter Four

Larry peeked at the neon Heiniken clock mounted over the backbar mirror. Thirty-two yawning minutes before he could catch a buzz. His impatient glance, coming less than a minute since the last look, deepened into a scowl. He'd violated the first rule of dealing drugs: don't use your own product. One call, a trip to Rockford, and handing over his very last cent had scored him a half-pound. He'd held out for less than twenty-four hours, and in the couple days since, his usage escalated to where it was already in danger of becoming a habit.

His empty stomach rumbled. Wanting to prolong his pre-shift buzz, he hadn't eaten since breakfast, and now the munchies were hollowing him out. Once he started eating, he knew he wouldn't stop until his belly hurt, and he preferred to keep that kind of gluttony private.

He edged toward the backroom doorway. A couple one-hitters would keep the munchies at bay until he got home. So far, he hadn't been able to work up the nerve to toke at work, even when the bar was empty. He kept flashing back to that day near the end of his senior year, when Coach Gaston busted him and his buds for smoking weed, even after they'd fogged the locker room with Lysol. Only his mortified parents' appeals kept him from being expelled. He couldn't afford to lose this job.

He lit a cigarette and took a shallow drag, which forced a gummy cough out of him. His lungs were cashed. For him, pot and nicotine went together like peanut butter and jelly. He was already smoking over a pack a day.

He crushed out the cigarette in an ashtray. He massaged his forehead. It wasn't supposed to go like this. But the pot just sat there tempting him. Desperate to get going, he'd dared two deals, both quarter ounces to dudes a bit on the shifty side. He couldn't see such risks leading to children and the white picket fence, only to prison bars. Maybe, if he managed to sell off the rest of his stash without getting arrested, he'd search for another way out of his financial mess.

16

He peered at the Heiniken clock. Thirty-one minutes to go. The front door swung open and a reflexive aversion saved his night vision as sunlight seared into the bar's dim cool. Margaret's fans were dribbling in, pretending to mull over what they were gonna order, but really just claiming their stools along the bar and hoarding their cash until she breezed in.

The newcomer screeched out the stool in front of Larry, who considering carding the dude. Larry had seen taller fourth graders. The newcomer's faded black Iron Maiden tee shirt and stringy, sweaty, long brown hair did nothing to suggest lawful maturity. His patchy, goatish beard made him look like a high schooler shooting for Wisconsin legal, but the deep droop of the bags under the dude's bloodshot eyes convinced Larry to forego carding the burnout.

"WhatcanIgetcha?" Larry asked.

"Can you make a Pina Colada?"

Larry was on the edge of claiming that the blender was broken, but he decided that making the fru-fru cocktail and re-cleaning zones he'd already cleaned would kill the clock.

When Larry placed the burnout's change on the bar, the dude tongued the straw out of his mouth and murmured, "I hear you can score."

Larry's breath hitched, but not loud enough, he thought, to put a dent in his outward cool. He returned the burnout's eager stare with a blank one of his own. One of those two dirtbags had fucked him over, after he specifically warned them not to tell anybody. By now the word might've spread throughout the druggy grapevine. This burnout might be just the tip of the lowlife iceberg, and was definitely not an example of the discrete blue-collar users he hoped to reach. He figured he'd get pretty good at pretending he didn't have any idea of what inquiring weed-freaks were talking about.

Behind Larry, from past the bend and near the end of the bartop's longer leg, a gruff voice called, "You fellas smell that?"

The burnout dipped his shaggy head and raised his shoulders. His eyes narrowed, but his voice wavered through high-pitched, friendly tones as he said, "Hey, Gene, what's up?"

Larry relaxed a bit. It sounded like the semi-vicious ribbing of friends, nothing that required his involvement.

Gene hollered, "Smells like pig shit."

17

Amidst the smattering of cruel chuckles, the burnout managed a wincing smile. Larry held his breath. His pulse quickened and tapped at his eardrums. He doubted that the burnout would try anything, what with Gene having about a foot and at least a hundred pounds on him, but he didn't know about Gene, one of those pervy loiterers that showed up a little early to nab a ringside seat for Margaret's shifts.

"No," Gene said, "it smells worse than pig shit." He inhaled loud through his nose while performing a few upward arcs of his palm, wafting the air towards himself. "What is that fragrance? It smells like … like *chicken pussy*."

Laughter erupted all over the barroom, the most intense explosions from those around Gene. The burnout, his head tilted downward so that Larry couldn't see his eyes, inched sideways, as if he was about to bolt for the front door.

Gene, a shit-eating grin on his face, hooted above the flagging laughter, saying, "Slappy, your dick so small you can fuck a chicken?"

The rollicking redoubled. Slappy, Larry guessed was the poor burnout's name, seemed to shrink further. He looked up at Larry, and, with shiny eyes, said, "It ain't true."

A sour aftertaste flooded Larry's mouth. He balled up his fists. "You stay put." He marched down in front of Gene. "Shut up or I'll kick your ass out for a month."

Gene's grin flattened, and his tiny eyes shocked as wide as they would go. No hitting on Margaret for a whole month appeared to be an even more powerful threat than Larry figured. Gene's fleshy cheeks reddened and his eyelids slitted. Larry knew the bully had to prove he wasn't chickenshit to his suddenly silent buddies. Larry, unblinking, leaned towards Gene. Up the bar, somebody called for a beer.

Larry held his glower for a second longer, then went back to work. He kept an eye on Slappy, who continued to sip his Pina Colada in virtual solitude, even as the crowd simmered up towards normal happy-hour boisterousness. Larry began to weigh the possibility that whichever dude had told Slappy that he could score also considered Slappy trustworthy.

When Slappy sucked his cocktail down to the dregs, Larry swung over and said, "Another?"

Slappy shook his head. "I oughtta jet."

"Listen, if that asshole doesn't like you, that makes you okay in my book." Larry glanced side to side. "I know a guy, but he doesn't want his name getting out. You tell me how much you want, I can have it for you tomorrow."

Slappy straightened up.

"Come by the bar," Larry said, "early, with the money, and that's that."

After settling the terms, Slappy handed Larry a homemade flier. "Party out at our place. Beer, pig roast, you should come."

Larry folded up the flier and stuck it into the back pocket of his jeans without looking at it. "Maybe. Just keep it to yourself, you know."

Larry, watching Slappy's enthusiastic nodding, told himself to chill out. He could always make this a one-time thing. He returned to the fruitless task of trolling for drink orders.

Margaret's arrival inspired the usual lift in the general mood. She made her way through the tables and along the outer bar, saying her hellos, favoring a few here and there with a light touch of the shoulder or a pat on the back.

"Ain't she a fox," Slappy said.

Larry pivoted, and gathering up his cigarettes and lighter, he snorted at his own half-googly reaction to her entrance. For one thing, she always wore sneakers, jeans, and a tee shirt, nothing sexpot, all girl-next-door. Secondly, everybody and their brother was chasing her. And lastly, he had no business getting all crushy about a girl so soon after his tragic affair with Deanne. Still, he popped a stick of Doublemint into his mouth to cover his motorbreath.

She shot him a little smile, then cruised into the backroom. Every darn time she greeted him with that same little smile. He couldn't decide if it was shy or just the bare-minimum acknowledgment of an insignificant coworker. Or something in between.

She popped out of the backroom, and, with a slight frown, said, "Didn't the snack order come today?"

A sharp twinge flexed behind his brow. "Damn, I forgot to bring up the sacks. Just gimme a sec."

"Thank you."

He piled his things beside the cash register and hustled down the backstairs. He blamed his forgetfulness on the weed. While toting a pair of industrial-sized sacks of nuts upstairs, he strained to exaggerate Margaret's annoyance into bitchiness of Deanne-like proportions.

When he returned to the front of the house, Margaret was chatting with Slappy, who, stirring his fresh Pina Colada, said, "After he scores for me, I'll turn you on …"

Larry rushed over, sputtering, "Hey, hey …" He floundered for something to say as blood scorched into his cheeks.

Margaret looked at him funny. "Ah, 'hey' what?"

Larry flashed a silent, be-cool plea at Slappy, who continued to bask in Margaret's presence. "I brought up the nuts."

Margaret's green eyes fixed on Larry. "Slappy's getting some Maiden *tickets*, and offered me one, but I have to work that night. But your nights are free, aren't they?"

His mouth gone dry, Larry mumbled a noncommittal reply to Slappy's instantaneous offer while enduring Margaret's scrutiny. *She knew.*

Margaret placed her palms on his pecs, then pushed. "Now get out of my way. Time for this chick to make the cheddar."

On the way to the door, Larry hoped his slow gait disguised his shaky knees. He tried to tease out a coherent line of thought from the tangle of questions. He was pretty sure that women didn't fondle dudes' chests for no good reason. But that meant that she didn't care about the pot. *Maybe*, she didn't know that he dealt. As he opened the door he stole a last look at the bar. Slappy hunched over his Pina Colada, sucking it dry. That stoner would tell her anything to impress her. Larry stepped out into the harsh sunlight, letting the door slam shut behind him.

Chapter Five

The forenoon sunlight glared against the right side of Larry's face. He bowed his head and aimed his eyes at the grainy sidewalk, certain that his droopy eyelids were a dead giveaway that he was baked out of his skull. He coughed up a wisp of smoke, the residue of the last toke he snuck beside house, next to the squirrel traps, before starting the walk to work.

About a block and a half out he crested the final hill along the way and gazed toward the town square. He stutter-stepped, then resumed his stride. Slappy, slouching against the pub's locked door, lit a cigarette.

Larry hissed in a breath. Lurking around, waiting for the bar to open, Slappy couldn't look more suspicious if he tried. Larry blamed himself, for not being specific about the time, for assuming that a stoner would know better. Talk about buzzkill. Instead of sailing through the first half, now he'd have to drag ass through the entire shift, worrying all the while if anybody would put two and two together.

Slappy turned his head towards Larry and sunlight dazzled off his mirrored shades. Larry shielded his eyes and saw that even though the loiterer was short enough, and his hair was long enough and the right shade of oily brown, he wasn't Slappy. Going by the sunglasses, the handlebar mustache, and the fuzzy sideburns, Larry recognized the asshole he'd thrown out of Bub's when he'd applied for the job.

Couldn't be.

Larry slowed. The asshole would have to be crazy to try to jump him in broad daylight on the town square. He must not know that Larry got the job. Larry nodded. He considered circling the block and going in the backdoor. If he was extra quiet, maybe by the time he finished the daily setup the little jerk would be gone.

The asshole shifted towards Larry and crossed his skinny arms over his puffed chest. Larry groaned. That asshole had spotted him, and, he didn't doubt, knew exactly who he was.

Larry picked up his pace. He might as well get it over with. When he was a couple storefronts away, the asshole flicked his cigarette into the gutter, then recrossed his arms. He jutted his chin, clean-shaven and displaying the twin slanted white scars, at Larry. He wore the same frayed, sleeveless jean jacket, the same sallow tee shit, probably the same scuzzy jeans, and the same shabby sneakers.

Larry stopped just out of arm's reach and angled himself slightly, in case he had to evade a sucker punch. He took a shallow breath, inhaling the same sour B.O. the asshole exuded last time. "You waiting for the pub to open?"

"You must be Larry."

"That's me."

"I'm Barney. Slappy's cousin. I'm s'posed to pick something up for him."

Larry frowned. He'd had no idea that Slappy was one of the infamous Heller Boys. "Where's Slappy?"

Barney tilted his head down and the whites of his eyes showed over his mirrored shades' rims. "Slappy's laying low right now. That a problem?"

Larry willed his facial muscles to full relaxation. Now a dude he'd humiliated knew a little about his illegal business. He could lie, nip this crap in the bud, but then again, he didn't need to sell much to break even and get out of this racket once and for all. Anyways, he supposed the damage was already done, what with Slappy telling Barney, and presumably, the rest of the Heller Boys, and with Barney sniffing around the closed pub waiting for him to show up. "I guess not." Twisting his torso enough to keep an eye on Barney, Larry stuck his key into the lock.

"So where is it?" Barney asked.

Larry, through gritted his teeth, answered, "*Not here*. Come inside where there's not so many eyeballs."

After the door was shut and locked behind them, Larry pulled the quarter ounce from his front pocket and handed it to Barney, who unrolled the baggy and held it up in front of his eyes. A good two fingers of weed bulged the baggie's bottom. "Don't look like much," Barney said.

"I weighed it myself. Slappy has a problem with it, he can let me know. Stash it, will ya?"

Barney re-rolled the baggie and crotched it.

Larry unlocked the door. "You'd better stick around for a little while or it'll look funny."

"Paranoid motherfucker, ain'tcha?"

"Just careful."

Larry went around flicking on the lights. Barney scuffed an upended stool down from the bartop and banged its legs against the floor. "Might as well set me up a beer."

Larry zipped behind the bar. "What'll you have?"

"Tap Murray's."

Larry scooped a mug under the spigot while pulling the tap-handle of the local brew. As always, the hollow sputter of an emptied keg gave too little warning, and foam spurted out of the spigot, spritzing a radius which included the bartop, the mug, and Larry's arm, before he could smack the tap-handle off.

Barney snickered.

Larry glared at the tap as he wiped spume off his arm. Normally, he'd check the taproom for dead kegs before opening. Now the little scumbag was laughing at him like he was a rookie bartender. "Tap's fried. You want a bottle?"

"Ugh. I *hate* it in the bottle."

Larry remembered Barney ordering bottles the last time they met, but he kept his mouth shut.

Barney drummed his fingers on the bartop, then said, "You gotta change the keg, right?"

No way was Larry gonna leave Barney alone while he went downstairs to change the keg. "I gotta wait for Bub to come in. I don't have keys to the basement."

Barney lowered his head and showed the whites of his eyes over his mirrored shades' rims again. Larry suppressed the urge to laugh in his face. Barney sucked his front teeth, making a long spitty noise, then leaned back from his 'scary' stare. "I guess I'll take a bottle."

While Larry popped the cap he was sure he heard Barney mutter, "Asshole." Larry placed the bottle a few inches to Barney's left, so that the little jerk would have to reach for it, then he hustled out from behind the bar and set to flipping chairs down from table tops.

The burble of a tipped beer bottle preceded Barney mumbling, "Gross." A moment later, the unmistakable metallic scrape of a Zippo led to the day's first cloud of secondhand smoke. Larry could've darted back behind the bar, but he continued to pull chairs down from tables. Barney griped, "You got an ashtray in this dump?"

Larry knew it was coming but he tensed up anyways. He speed-walked behind the bar. He grabbed a stack of clear glass ashtrays and slid one spinning down the bartop, the ashtray quivering to a stop next to Barney's elbow. Larry had ashtrays on half of the tables when Barney yelled, "You got any nuts?"

Larry huffed a barely audible *shhh*. The little jerk had to be doing it on purpose. As he returned to the bar he kept telling himself that the best revenge was to show no signs of aggravation. He placed a wooden bowl of mixed nuts in front of Barney, who sifted through the lesser nuts and picked out cashews. Larry noticed the grime blackening Barney's cuticles and made a mental note to toss the remaining nuts after the jerk left.

Larry was settling in behind the bar when Barney tipped his beer, and his head, all the way back, holding that pose until he got every last drop, then he *tocked* the empty bottle down on the bartop. He placed his palms on the rail, but didn't push to his feet.

Behind his back, Larry crossed his fingers against Barney ordering another beer.

"Slappy said he invited you to the big shindig," Barney said. "You gonna show?"

"I dunno." He'd heard enough about the Heller Boys to suspect that Barney might try to lure him out to where they could bushwhack him.

"Listen, the other day, I was pretty fucking wasted. Shouldn't've been here in the first place. I say let bygones be bygones. No hard feelings?"

"No. No hard feelings." Larry didn't buy it. For one thing, Barney made no move to shake hands.

Barney leaned back, his nose up in the air. "Yeah, ever since I bagged and tagged that bitch, she's had it in for me. Guess she's pissed I never called her after." He shrugged. "What can I say? She's a dead lay."

Larry squinted, but he held his tongue. He didn't see any point in calling the asshole on his obvious lie.

Barney stood up from the stool. "Anyways, you oughtta come out. A guy holding could make a lotta cash."

"I hear things are dry."

24

"Dryer than dust." Barney swaggered to the door.

"I'll see if I can make it."

As the Barney went through the door, Larry could've sworn he muttered something that sounded like, '*Bite the root.*'

Chapter Six

Under the dim green glow of the Olds' dashlights Larry studied the map scrawled on the crinkled flier. Slappy's directions followed straight lines and right angles labeled with legible names of roads and with arrows tracing the route from Murray to the party. Slappy's directions bore little relation to reality. Larry had leaned into looping curves and fishtailed around switchbacks. He'd driven through several unmarked intersections. The last road sign he saw was a half an hour back when he'd left pavement for gravel. Twice now he'd dead-ended, once turning up the lane of a darkened and apparently foreclosed farm.

He surveyed the countryside. Dense ranks of corn rolled to each black horizon. He shook his head. He'd blow the whole stupid thing off and go home if he had any idea where he was. He figured if he kept traveling south, sooner or later he had to hit a main road.

He crested a sharp rise. A red reflector, mounted on a white mailbox, flared against the beams of the Olds' headlights. The fields remained a dark green expanse. He pulled up next to the mailbox. A dirt lane snaked into the corn. Distorted death-metal, transmitting from a ways down the lane, buzzed over the rumble of the Olds' idling engine.

He balled up the map and tossed it onto backseat floorboards. He thrummed his fingers against the steering wheel. The Heller Boys might be waiting to beat the shit out of him. But even if things went smooth, and he managed to take enough orders to sell off his stash and be done with dealing once and for all, who knew how long he'd have to put up with born-to-lose types showing up at the bar looking for weed.

He glanced at the paper grocery bag sitting on the passenger seat. He'd brought his own booze. He'd already come this far. If the Hellers wanted to kick his ass, they didn't need to lure him out to the middle of nowhere to do it. And all he had to do was tell dudes his source got busted, and that would be the end of that.

He whispered, "Suck it up, man. It'll be over before you know it." He guided the Olds onto the dirt lane.

He spotted parked cars as soon as he rounded the first bend. He pulled in well behind the nearest one, leaving the Olds tilted partway into the weedy ditch. As he toted the grocery bag up the lane the frenetic music grew louder, and the cars lining the lane grew denser.

Cruel laughter chattered from a couple cars ahead on his right. The orange coals of their cigarettes tinged the murky shapes slouching around the bed of a pickup. They fell silent as he approached them. He nodded in their general direction. Nobody said a word as he came abreast, but coarse chuckles soughed at his back. He struggled to maintain a cool pace.

The lane twisted through the corn to a farmstead. Darkness shrouded the canted farmhouse's upper story, but the ground-floor windows glowed red, limning clumps of milling partygoers. A thrashing pack of longhairs headbanged and moshed to the devilish riffs of Slayer. More casual groups clustered around the front yard. Some guys leaned against an El Camino and a double-decker camper truck, others sat under the giant leafless oak that loomed over the small house. Everybody gripped plastic disposal cups. Most of these groups were one hundred percent male, although half a dozen or so girls huddled together under the huge tree, with a thick ring of dudes surrounding them. A jumble of barns stood beyond the house, with a massive, hanger-like structure dwarfing the more quaint buildings closer to the house. Beyond the barns corn swayed as far as the eye could see.

Larry weaved his way through partygoers. AC/DC, the Bon Scott version, replaced Slayer, the people nearest to the house shouting over the bruising power chords. Larry followed the walkway to a sagging screen door. Paint peeled in long, dirty white strips from the wall around the doorway.

Larry stepped inside. Hazy red light seeped through a door ajar on the adjacent wall, tinting the small porch with bloody shadows. A metal washtub containing two kegs dominated the cement floor. Low and against the far wall, guarding the kegs and the open door, on a Naugahyde bench seat stripped from the back of some junker, Slappy sulked with his short legs sprawled out and his arms crossed over his chest.

When the screen door banged shut behind Larry, Slappy looked up and leaped from his seat. "Dude!" He clamped Larry's outstretched hand and pumped. Larry feared Slappy might separate his shoulder. Slappy guided him towards the kegs. "Lemme get you a beer."

Larry hefted the grocery sack. "Brought my own. Smirnoff-OJ" He eyed the sloshy ice water in the tub. "I just need a cup and some fresh ice."

Slappy ushered Larry through the door into a grubby kitchen. Slappy pointed Larry towards the fridge. Larry cleared a workspace on the cluttered counter. He found ice in the freezer and commenced to mixing a cocktail. Slappy disappeared into the next room, then returned with two dudes.

Slappy introduced his cousins, Mike and Bill. Mike, maybe an inch shorter than Larry, wore his long brown hair drawn tight into a ponytail. His sleeveless, green-and-blue checkered flannel showed off his baseball-sized biceps, and hung to the crotch of his faded jeans. Bill, as short as Slappy, wore his hair tucked underneath a dirty ballcap. A pair of tinted glasses obscured his eyes. A fuzzy brown beard and mustache snaggled down his cheeks and chin to the collar of his red tee shirt. The white-lettered Skoal logo flaked above the slight swell of his beer belly. Over Bill's shoulder, lurking in the red-lit room, Barney, in his wannabe-biker denim, stared towards Larry from behind his mirrored shades.

Mike shifted his sharp eyes toward Slappy. "Who's watching the kegs?"

Slappy huffed. He fished a roll of dollar bills out of his pocket and handed it to Bill, then returned to his post.

Mike winked at Larry. "C'mon."

The sturm and drang of AC/DC grew to ear-splitting levels as Larry followed Mike and Bill into the red room. The evil glow radiated from pair of red bulbs, each screwed into a shadeless lamp, one of which sat on a scarred end table at the south end of a battered couch. The other radiated at the opposite side of the room on a stool next to a tri-level, homemade, cinder-block-and-bare-plank shelving unit. The shelves housed a sleek black stereo system and a couple stacks of record albums. More records littered the warped hardwood floor, and a few balanced on top of the uneven heap of junk crowding the coffee table. Barney and three other dudes each brandished an album while clustering around the stereo.

28

Mike shook his index finger at Barney and the other dudes. "Turn that shit down! Now!"

Barney regarded Mike while Malcolm Young bashed through a few more chords, then he nudged the volume knob down a hair.

The din falling just below shouting level, Mike gave one last finger shake to Barney. "You blow them speakers you're gonna buy new ones." He gestured for Larry to take a seat in a barcalounger, its ratty fabric held together by strips of duct tape. Mike plopped down on the couch. "God I hate AC/DC."

Larry nodded, even though he dug the Bon Scott version. He sat down on the bulgy barcalounger. A huge Judas Priest poster, the band posing over their logo in their heavy metal leather gear, covered the portion of the north wall between a pair of windows. A speaker, aimed outside, filled each open window. At the other end of the coffee table a three-quarter sized Cort bass reclined in a guitar stand, scars marring the bass's red lacquer, the two outer strings missing from its gummy fretboard. To Larry's left an ancient and dusty console TV faced the couch. A bunny-ears antenna mechanism sat on top of the console. Among the party debris on the coffee table, butts smoked down to the filter overflowed a frisbee-shaped glass ashtray. A fan on the windowsill near Larry's head blew outward, but its dust-caked blades did little to relieve the whiff of stale Fritos permeating the room.

Bill sat on the other side of Mike, who said, "Somebody go get Precious."

The smallest member of Barney's crew dropped the album he was holding and, betraying a slight limp, hurried out of the room. Barney remained by the stereo. The other two, one of them rubbing his hands together, dragged kitchen chairs over to the coffee table, and sat opposite from the couch.

Mike waved a hand at the duo. "This is Jay-Jay and Jackie. They're identical twins."

Larry didn't need Mike to tell him that. They had the same unkempt, long brown hair that all the Hellers seemed to prefer. Larry hadn't caught which was which, but one of them wore Metallica's infamous Metal Up Your Ass tee shirt, depicting a hand wielding a knife while rising out of a toilet. This twin had rolled the tee shirt's long sleeves up to his elbows, exposing a pair of bony forearms. The other twin went shirtless, revealing a torso so lean that his washboard abs extended to an eight-pack. A skull and crossbones tattoo, green and faded, blotted his right deltoid. He wore a pair of jeans cut off and frayed at the knees. Otherwise, they were identical, right down to their crooked noses and the purplish bags under their eyes.

They barely nodded at Larry, instead focusing on Mike, who produced a baggie of pot. He dumped a small pile on the cover of a magazine. He went to work sifting out the stems and seeds. Even in the dim red light Larry recognized his brand of dope.

The smallest Heller returned to the room carrying a ridiculously long bong. Mike looked up from his work. "Bring her over, Looey."

Going by Looey's hairless babyface, Larry estimated him to be a freshman at best, years younger than anybody else in the room. In contrast to the other Hellers, his clothes seemed fairly new, the black of his Motley Crüe tee shirt still deep, its logo still intact. His jeans were dark and stiff, and his sneakers unwrinkled. Other than his slight limp, he appeared hale and hearty, especially next to his elder kin, who all, except for Mike, looked sallow and … *infectious*.

Looey handed Precious to Mike, who began to load the bowl. Precious was five feet of translucent PVC pipe, probably red, but Larry wasn't sure if the plastic was only absorbing the ambient light.

Mike handed Precious, armed and ready, to Larry. "Guests first."

Larry pulled out his Bic, but there was no way he could toke while lighting the bowl, which was a few inches from the pipe's opposite end. Barney slid over. "I got it."

Larry didn't like Barney's wicked grin. Barney knelt by the bottom of Precious and flicked his Zippo. Larry emptied his lungs, then began to draw on the open end of the bong. Barney took his lighter away once the weed started to burn. Larry watched the smoke curl up inside the pipe. When he figured he had about half a lung left, he pointed at Barney to pull the stem so he could shotgun the smoke.

"C'mon," Barney said, "just a little more to go."

The pot glowed orange, the bowl nowhere near cashed.

"Don't be a pussy," Barney said. "C'mon!"

Larry's pulse throbbed in his temples. He snapped his fingers twice, and still Barney didn't pull the stem. Larry could have stopped and covered the open end of the bong with his hand, trapping the smoke inside while he took a fresh breath, but they were all watching him, the twins snickering, Barney grinning wider, baring his mottled teeth.

The bowl finally burned out. Barney pulled the stem, and Larry gave it all he had, sucking the pipeful of smoke into his lungs. A few smoky tendrils coiled out of the bong after he leaned back and clamped his mouth shut.

For a second, everybody was silent, with AC/DC chugging away in the background, and then the smoke in Larry's lungs expanded. Violent coughs exploded up from the depths of his lungs, wracking his body, rending his throat. With each hack, the cloud of smoke around him grew larger. He bent over, put his head between his knees, and gasped for breath. He thought he was gonna puke.

Meanwhile, they laughed and they laughed. Somebody clapped him on the back. He eased in breaths to the coughing point, which slowly receded. He sat up when he could take a full breath. The bong was already three guys down the circle. He found his cocktail and took a long drink.

Mike shrugged. "You gotta respect Precious."

Larry sat back and let the buzz roll up on him. When the bong came around again, he waved it away. Barney replaced AC/DC with Rush's first live album, the one without any keyboard crap on it. Larry began to hover for an opening in the conversation, so he could tell the Hellers his connection had dried up, and after that, he'd get the hell out of Dodge.

The shirtless twin caught Larry's eye. "You work at Bub's, right?"

Larry nodded.

"So you know Margaret."

"Yeah, I know her."

"I fucked that bitch."

Barney and the other twin cracked up. Larry's jawbone twitched.

"Shut the fuck up," Mike said. "She wouldn't let a loser like you touch her with a ten foot pole."

The shirtless twin scowled. Larry bowed his head to hide his smile.

Mike stood up. "Why don't you guys get the fuck out of here, go keep an eye on things outside."

Barney was the last to stand. His mirrored shades reflected red light before he spun and followed the others out of the room. Larry levered himself up from the barcalounger, unsure whether or not he was being dismissed too. Bill hung back with Mike, who gave a light backhand to Larry's bicep and said, "Let's go upstairs where we can hear each other talk."

Larry followed them up a narrow stairwell. The rickety steps sagged under his soles. The wall on his left slanted inward, reducing the passage so that his shoulders grazed both walls. Mike and Bill stopped on the dark landing. They'd traveled far enough so that they could speak in normal tones over the jammed-out live version of *Working Man*.

Mike faced Larry. Bill stood behind Mike's left shoulder. Larry took a breath and opened his mouth, the lie about his dried-up connection on the tip of his tongue.

"We want to partner up with you," Mike said.

Larry blinked. "I don't–"

"Slappy told us all about your setup," Mike said. "You think you're the first guy to try that scam?"

Larry's tongue puckered in his bone-dry mouth.

"Chill out, man," Mike said. "We got a scam of our own, and nobody needs to be the wiser."

"What scam?"

Mike sniffed. "Obviously you got a good connection. We want you to supply us, that's all. Totally low risk."

"I, I don't know."

"All you gotta do is walk the stuff to us. Quarter pounds, maybe halfs, nothing bigger than that. We'll handle the distribution. We already know every stoner in the county. We'll take care of the country mice, and you can do your thing in Murray, and never the tween shall meet."

Larry did some hasty calculations. "I'm gonna have to think about it."

"Tell ya what," Mike said. "You do this for us, and I'll keep Barney and Slappy and the rest of them away from your bar." He cradled his right fist in his left palm. "Otherwise, the cops, you know, we got us a reputation. They're gonna wonder why my cousins are all of sudden regulars at Bub's."

Larry flailed for something other to say than 'Yes.' This deal was going down way too damned fast. "Why don't you guys just grow your own?"

Mike smiled. "You don't think we thought of that? It takes too long. It's too much trouble. And even if you're lucky enough to get a crop in, nine times out of ten, it turns out to be Illinois Green."

"Yeah," Bill said, "and if the cops find a patch, they stake it out and bust you when you show up to water it or whatever. It's too much fuckin' trouble."

"So there it is," Mike said. "What's to think about? You pick up a little more, and you make a lot more money. It's win-win for everybody."

On the dark landing Larry couldn't see well enough to judge Mike's eyes. He doubted that Mike was above making an anonymous phone call to the cops. He nodded.

"Good." Mike shifted his open palm towards Bill, who slapped a roll of bills in his hand. Mike handed the damp wad of cash to Larry. "That's a down payment on the first run. Work out the details with Bill. You'll be dealing with him from now on." He clapped his hands. "Good. We're all set." He stepped around Larry and bounded down the stairs.

Bill fingered the tip of his brambly beard. "Let's talk."

By the time they stepped outside, Larry holding a fresh screwdriver, the two of them had hammered out the details. Bill excused himself. Larry meandered, hunting for a familiar face, but he found nobody but Hellers and high school kids. He ended up taking a seat on an overturned tractor tire near the barns. He smoked a cigarette and watched dudes act like idiots in order to impress the scarce girls. He decided that as soon as he saw a friendly Heller, he'd say his goodbyes and head on home. He'd leave the attempt to figure a way out of his new partnership until tomorrow.

He was on his second cigarette and down to the slush of his screwdriver when a girl disengaged from a clique near the house and marched toward him. On a dare, he supposed. On each determined footfall her grapefruit-sized boobs threatened to jiggle out of her snow white tank-top. Her jean shorts rode high on her thighs, her sneakers gleamed as white as her skin-tight top. She loomed in front of him, crossing her arms under her breasts. He put her at five-five or so. The tips of her straight dark hair brushed her shoulders. She wore her bangs swept back and tucked behind her ears. Her hostile expression only made her small eyes, small nose, and small mouth cuter. She demanded, "Who invited you?"

Larry smirked. "Who wants to know?"

Her scowl deepened. "I'm gonna ask you one more time, smartass."

Larry stood. She held her ground, though she had to tilt her head upwards to maintain eye contact. He said, "Who invited *you*?"

"My brother Mike lives here. *That's who*. If I snap my fingers about twenty guys will kick your ass in two seconds flat."

"What's goin' on?"

Larry twisted around. Mike strode out of the deeper shadows of the barns. Larry jabbed his thumb toward his interrogator. "I think she's trying to kick me out of the party."

Mike slung an arm over Larry's shoulder. "Is that true, Meryl?"

"A girl named Meryl," Larry said. "Is that like a boy named Sue?"

Mike laughed. Larry couldn't be sure in the dark, but he was pretty sure that Meryl blushed. Mike walked over to her and put his arm around her shoulder. "This little hellion's my little sister. Sis, this is Larry, the guest of honor."

Meryl shrugged out from under Mike's arm and took a step to the side.

Mike chuckled. "You better look out for this one. She be man crazy."

Meryl snarled, then stomped away.

Mike shook, then wiped his eyes. "She's a good kid, but she's kind of a flirt. You see the way she dresses?"

While Mike watched him, Larry willed himself not to steal a glance at her ass.

"C'mon," Mike said. "Looks like you need a refill."

Mike started toward the house. Larry trailed behind Mike while steeling himself to say that he'd better get going. Halfway to the house, somebody hollered, "Cops!"

Panic ensued. There were more shouts of 'Cops!' People scattered, some stumbling, some falling, everyone spilling beer. A single whoop of a police siren preceded the appearance of the flashing red lights of two patrol cars cruising up the lane.

"Hang loose," Mike said. He strolled into the house like nothing was happening. Moments later, the volume of the music dipped to a nearly inaudible level.

Bill appeared beside Larry. "Just relax. They do this every goddamned time."

"What about all these kids?"

"Everybody knows the drill. You got ID, right?"

"Yeah, sure. But I also got weed on me."

"So be cool, all they're gonna check is if you're old enough to be drinking."

Larry surveyed the corn. In every region tassels bobbed, stalks rustled, and runaways giggled and whispered abrupt commands to each other. "It's like shooting fish in a barrel."

"Just chill. Don't talk to them unless they ask you a question."

Mike moseyed out of the house and stood on the other side of Bill. They watched the patrol cars roll to a stop. Larry couldn't see how they'd explain the difference between the dozen or remaining dudes, who all tried to look nonchalant, and the dozens of cars parked bumper to bumper along the lane.

"County boys," Mike said, "just like usual."

Larry took a deep breath. A cop got out of each cruiser, the lights still flashing, and the two of them sauntered up toward Mike, who said, "Officer Wells, Officer Burgett, how's it hangin'?"

The older of the two cops, his great belly straining against his uniform shirt and sagging over his belt, stopped in front of Mike. "That's 'Sergeant Wells,' Michael." The younger cop busied himself snooping around the house and peeking in windows.

"My mistake, Sergeant."

"You make it every time, Michael. Keep it up and I'm gonna start thinking that you're fucking with me." Sergeant Wells scanned the yard. "Having a little party, are we?"

"Just getting primed for Cheese Days. It's right around the corner, ya know."

Sergeant Wells rubbed his forehead. "Christ, don't remind me." He gazed over the corn. "Any minors out there?"

"No sir, we're all legal."

Officer Burgett wandered back to the group and paused in front of Larry. He shined his flashlight in Larry's face. "Who might you be? You a brand new Heller?"

"He's a friend of ours," Bill said. "From Murray. He works at Bub's."

"Is that so?" Officer Burgett asked. "You got ID?"

Larry shaded his eyes with one hand and pulled out his wallet with the other. He handed Officer Burgett the yellow receipt they gave him when they took his license.

Officer Burgett shined his flashlight on the ticket. "Dee-double-yoo-eye, eh? From Wisconsin? I thought you were from Murray."

Larry, seeing spots, said, "I moved a couple of months ago."

Officer Burgett handed the ticket back. "You better not be driving drunk with this hanging over your head."

"Yes sir."

Officer Burgett gave Larry one more faceful of his flashlight's beam before roaming away.

Sergeant Wells eyed his partner, then said, "So where's your cousin?"

Mike scratched his head. "Slappy? I ain't seen him for a while."

"He out at your mom's?"

"Not as far as I know. Last time I saw him, I told him to turn himself in."

"The longer he hides out, the worse it's gonna be."

Mike nodded. "Next time I see him, maybe I'll just tie him up and bring him in myself."

Sergeant Wells snorted. "All right." He looked at the cars parked up and down the lane. "Nobody drives home drunk, then we got no problems. Got it?"

"Got it."

Sergeant Wells shook his head and ambled back to his car. Officer Burgett followed.

Mike called out, "Thanks, Sergeant."

The three of them stood still until the patrol cars disappeared around the bend. A runnel of sweat ran from Larry's armpit ran down his ribs. The cops seemed awful familiar with his new business partners.

Mike walked back in the house. The tunes roared back up to the previous blaring volume. Drunken minors began to stumble out of the corn. Larry turned to Bill. "Why are they after Slappy?"

Bill itched his bearded jawline. "Long story short, he fucked up big time, got himself arrested, then skipped the court date."

"He skipped the date?"

"He was fucked either way. They could make a case that he stole a state cop's private vehicle, on top of drunk driving."

Larry frowned. "They could make a case?"

"If they wanted to. What really happened was, well, he more or less borrowed this kid's car, and it just happened to be his dad's car, and the dad just happens to be a state trooper. The kid was sort of passed out, and Slappy woke him up and said he had to move the kid's car, so he gave Slappy the keys, and then Slappy decided to take it for a little joyride."

"And he got pulled over."

"Bingo. So now they got him for failure to appear, contempt of court, whatever they call it, on top of everything else."

"Didn't he know the kid's dad was a cop?"

"Sure." Bill shrugged. "He was drunk."

Larry laughed.

"So they come by once a week or so," Bill said, "sniffing around for him."

"He should just turn himself in. Does he think he can duck them forever?"

"They'll never catch him." Bill craned his neck while looking towards the corn. Larry followed his gaze and saw a trio of guys emerging from the bordering stalks. "I gotta go talk to this dude."

Larry waited for Bill to walk away, then he hurried toward the house. Screw the goodbyes, he was gonna grab his booze and go while the gettin' was good. The kitchen was dark and deserted. Megadeth raged from the stereo in the next room. His grocery sack sat on the counter. As he reached for it, he sensed movement behind him. He whirled.

Meryl, standing close behind him, shifted from foot to foot while holding out an empty cup. "Can you make me one of those?"

Larry could barely hear her voice over the shredded guitar licks, but he got the gist. While he mixed the cocktail at the counter, she sidled up next to him and watched, her bare shoulder rubbing against his arm. He finished the drink and handed it to her, taking the opportunity to inch away. She took a sip, her eyes sparkling at him over the cup's rim.

Larry studied her fresh face and tried to assess her precise age, but, in the reddish shadows, he could do no more than ballpark it. At best she was eighteen. At worst, he'd get his ass kicked for fooling around with Mike's early-blooming kid sister.

She stepped forward and went up on tiptoes, her breasts grazing his chest, and she rasped in his ear, "I wanna show you something upstairs."

Her hot breath caused him to twitch down below. Her precise age didn't seem so important anymore. It had been months. Months and months.

"Bring the booze," she said.

On the way up he kept telling himself how stupid he was being. On the way up he kept looking behind himself to see if anybody was watching them climb the stairs. Past the upper landing she pulled him into a pitch black room. She let go of him and shut the door, reducing the thrash metal to a low rumble. The lock *snicked* home.

"Turn on a light," he said.

"They'll see it."

The curtains parted on the south-facing window. As his eyes adjusted to the feeble, indirect moonlight, he made out the shape of a twin bed. He took a swallow from the screwdriver, then set the drink, the vodka, and the carton of OJ down on the nightstand beside the bed.

She was on him in a flash. She forced his mouth open with her tongue. In a matter of seconds she had his jeans unbuttoned and unzipped and wide open. She pushed his underwear down. His cock stiffened rock-hard before she grabbed it. She disengaged her mouth from his and began to backpeddle, drawing him along with her.

She tugged him into a corner of the room, then she dropped down in a chair in front of him. Her mouth enveloped his penis. He moaned. It had been so long he'd forgotten what it felt like. Deanne hated doing it, made it obvious that she hated doing it while she was doing it, and always cut it short.

Meryl, on the other hand, was going at it with gusto. His toes curled in his boots. He closed his eyes, knowing that if he watched her bobbing head he wouldn't last much longer. Still, he couldn't ignore the rhythmic slurps, and closing his eyes just freed up more of his attention. He tried to think of baseball, he tried to do math in his head, but her accelerating strokes could not be ignored. In what seemed to him like a shamefully short amount of time, he had to say, "You'd better stop … I'm close."

With a wet *pop* she ejected his cock, and slightly out of breath, she said, "Yeah? Are you a one-and-done kind of guy?"

He shook his head. "Not tonight."

By the time they made it to the bed, they discovered that neither of them had a condom, but he was way past caring, and she didn't protest. He couldn't get enough of her. She let him do everything he wanted, things that no other woman had ever allowed him to do. Between his explorations of her firm curves and her playful aggression, he had no trouble performing encore after encore.

They were savoring a lull, sprawled and lounging in lazy caresses, the house now hushed, the party fizzling out sometime during their last go-round, when he, coasting along in a comfortable haze, gazed out the window.

With a jerk he sat up. He squeaked, "What the fuck?"

"What?"

He pointed at the window. Perched in profile on the sill outside, a figure darkened all of the bottom and half of the top pane. He squinted. The silhouette of a long tail swished up the thing's back.

Meryl sat up. "Goddamn it!" She pushed off of Larry and bounced out of the bed.

"What the fuck?"

While she stamped over to the window she snarled, "It's a goddamned squirrel." She whapped the windowpane. "Scat!"

"That can't be a squirrel!"

She smacked the window hard enough to rattle it in its frame. She yanked the curtains shut. In the sudden darkness the sound of claws scrabbling at the outside of the house decayed.

"No way was that a squirrel," Larry said. "That was a dude, in a fur coat, or a costume or some shit."

She padded back to the bed. She eased herself down on him, forcing him to his back. "They get big out here."

"No way, not that big. Anyways, what the hell was it doing?"

"Sometimes they try to get into the house." She kissed him, giving his lower lip a teasing nip. "So, you wanna talk about squirrels, or what?" She squeezed his limp dick. "Dang. I thought you were working back up to another one." She performed a series of deep strokes. He began to respond. She purred, "That's more like it."

He closed his eyes and sighed. A slight ache accompanied his growing erection. He guessed this time was gonna take a while. "Can I ask you a personal question?"

"Sure."

"How old are you?"

"Fourteen."

His froze mid-inhale.

She cackled, her entire body quaking. "Oh my god! I'm kidding! I'm eighteen! My brothers call me 'barely legal.'"

She let out a string of witchy giggles.

He let out a deep breath, then laughed.

Between giggles, she said, "Gotcha!"

He bit his lip. He seized her and her giggles grew to shrieks. He manhandled her, flipping her onto stomach and mounting her. He growled, "You're gonna pay for that."

She arched upwards. "Promises, promises."

Chapter Seven

A metallic bang jarred Larry awake. He whacked his knee into the bottom of the steering wheel. The hollow pain aggravated the greater agony dominating his head. Using Smirnoff-OJ's to replenish bodily fluids had seemed like a good idea through the long, draining night.

Highlights strobed across his mind. He smiled while moaning. He parted his eyelids. The sky was bluing. About the only thing he remembered from the drive home was the shallower shade of dark trimming the horizon. He had no idea why he decided to crash in the Olds rather than staggering the last thirty or so paces to his bed.

He yawned so wide his jaw popped. He wondered what had woke him up. He winced from the effort, but he was able to replay the noise in his head. He recognized the familiar clank of a squirrel trap slamming shut.

"Christ."

He closed his eyes. He belched, almost vomiting at the tail end of it. He didn't want to move. He also didn't want to puke in his car. He figured he'd better do it now, or that little bugger might be trapped until he woke again, which probably wouldn't be until afternoon. The Sunday morning hush lulled him. He caught himself drifting. He rubbed his eyes. Just five minutes more. A grating scrape made his drooping eyelids flutter.

He sat up straight. That scrape was too soft to be a slamming trapdoor. Only Reeves would be up this early. He frowned. He had to know.

He licked his lips and eased the door handle up until the catch released with a faint *thonk*. He lurched out of the car and steadied himself on the door, then shut the door with a muted click. He slipped over to the side of the house.

Mrs. Reeves had already crossed three-quarters of the yard. Her white sneakers flashed across the lush green grass. Her khakis and long-sleeved, yellow flower-print blouse rippled around her bony limbs. Normally straight-backed and shoulders squared, now her back humped, her head hunched, and the wide brim of her straw hat jounced with each step. On a red two-wheel dolly she carted one of the squirrel cages towards the Weeds.

He edged along the house and hunkered at its corner. She steered the dolly between two trees and disappeared into the Weeds. On the balls of his feet he dashed over the dewy lawn. He stopped at the two trees she'd passed between. A narrow dirt path slashed through the dense green tangle before vanishing into the shady depths.

A mosquito buzzed his ear. He whisked it away. He wondered how far she'd go. The racket of the waiting insect horde eroded his wonder. He was already sweating from the dash across the yard. The bugs would go nuts for his alcohol-saturated perspiration. Plus, he was no botanist, but he was pretty sure the spindly plants lining the trail were itchweed. And he had no clue what poison oak or poison ivy looked like.

The bags under his eyes throbbed and seemed to apply upward pressure on his lower eyelids. He needed sleep. He was about to turn back when he remembered her claim that she released the trapped squirrels in the park. That and her sneaky posture … He peered down the path.

He hustled, hoping to evade the lazier winged pests, but the requirements of stealth kept him well away from top speed. The unfamiliar route slowed him too, as the hardpack path meandered into the cool green haze, the leafy canopy above filtering the brightening daylight. The path angled past thickets of sun-starved and stunted saplings huddled between gnarled and mossy trunks of sporadic, hoary giants. He ducked low-hanging branches and fended off willowy switches.

After edging around a tree carbuncled by a bulging and teeming bee hive, which protruded from the bark just above his head, he reached the steep banks of the river. With a decent run-up he thought he might be able to vault to the opposite bank, but he wouldn't wanna risk plunging into the brown waters below. The yellow curds of foam swirling down the current were all the proof of toxicity that he needed.

A trail twice as wide as his ran parallel to the river. There were no wheel tracks in the bare dirt. He stood still. The bedlam of bug calls grated his nerves. He felt like they were signaling his position to one another as they closed in for the kill. He held his breath. From up the trail a raking *chuff* made him picture Reeves sliding the dolly out from under the cage.

He ducked down and took off. The wider trail allowed him to boogie faster. He slowed when he approached a tight path branching off the trail towards the river. From that direction, he heard the jangle of chain links ratcheting around a pulley. The path skirted an old growth tree with a silo-like trunk. He slunk toward the mechanical noises, flattening the entire sole of his boot on the dirt before putting any weight on each forward step. He stopped halfway around the tree, took a quick step back, hiding his body, then he edged forward far enough to see.

In a small clearing on a ledge overhanging the river, Mrs. Reeves was screwing a C-clamp shut. The clamp cinched to a flange welded to the middle of the cage's topside. Joined to the clamp, a slender chain slanted upward and outward to a winch, which hung over the river from a thick branch of the great tree. Off to the side, a yard-long aluminum pole with a hooked end leaned against the dolly.

The clamp fastened, Mrs. Reeves stepped back. The squirrel shivered in the center of the cage, its paws splayed on the cage floor. Mrs. Reeves grasped another chain, this one hanging from the dense leafage over solid ground. The chain looped at the bottom, creating two lines, and she began pulling one line down, hand over gloved hand.

The burring of links around pulley's drum accompanied the tautening of the chain clamped to the cage. The cage rose from the bare dirt and swung out into space. The cage pendulumed back and forth in a diminishing arc, finally settling into a position over the river. He gnashed his teeth. Scalding blood rushed into his face. His darkening field of vision shrank. A couple summers ago, he was drunk and he decided it would be cool to swim across a lake. Over halfway, the water went cold and muddy, and milfoil began to choke the surface. His friends ignored his screams for help because they thought he was fooling around.

His heartbeat thudded in his skull. His thick tongue squelched loose from the roof of his mouth. He found himself on his knees and clutching the crumbly bark of the huge tree.

The clink of the chains drew his attention. Mrs. Reeves reversed direction, and began lowering the cage. The squirrel darted back and forth, pawing the bars, until the cage dropped below the ledge and out of sight. Larry slid to the dirt behind the tree. He closed his eyes. He gasped silent breaths as deeply as he dared.

The burr of the winch broke the spell. It was too late to do anything now. He used the noise to mask his retreat as he skulked back to the house. He hurried up to his room and stood a little back from the north window. He had a full view of the far end of the backyard. She must've been doing it for years. Her late husband probably built the drowning machine, back when he was spry enough to climb trees.

She emerged from the Weeds, pushing the dolly. The empty, wet cage gleamed in the sunlight. Her black wraparound sunglasses, her manic scurry, made him take a step back. He needed rest, he needed to gather himself before he confronted her.

Chapter Eight

With the back of his hand Larry wiped away the sweat pooling over his upper lip. He'd planned on being halfway home by now, zooming down the road with the windows open and the breeze whipping through his hair, but Mike and Bill had insisted he come inside and smoke a doob.

Dust crusted the blades of the pair of lifeless fans mounted in the windows. When the blades were spinning the living room hadn't been half as stuffy, but Bill had ordered them switched off because he wanted to get right to work on the half-pound Larry had delivered. Bill wouldn't chance one single flake blowing away.

The rest of the Heller boys, except Slappy, had gathered to watch Bill weigh and measure eighths and quarters, and of course, to partake in the doobage. Bill and Mike took the couch, clearing the coffee table of everything except a box of baggies, a hand scale, the brick of marijuana, and the big, butt-heaped glass ashtray. Looey, wide-eyed, perched on an overturned milk crate right next to Bill, studied his elder's every move. On Looey's left, Barney claimed the barcalounger. He reclined impassive behind his mirrored shades. Larry sat on a rickety wooden kitchen chair on Barney's left, and on Larry's left, completing the circle, the shirtless twin, Jackie, Larry was pretty sure, sat hunchbacked on a barstool, then J.J on an old-timey chair that was little more than an aluminum frame and a red Naugahyde seat cushion. Motorhead raged away at a subdued volume on the stereo.

Larry looked past Barney, who was sucking on the joint. Dust coated the end table occupying the corner between the couch and the barcalounger. In fact, dust coated everything in the room, the TV's screen especially thick with it. The evening sun was shining on the other side of the house, but even in the premature twilight Larry spotted powdery dust bunnies peeking out from under the end table. Now he understood why the Hellers went with murky red light at the party: it was a helluva lot easier to mask the filth by switching a few bulbs than it was to actually clean the dump.

Barney passed the smoldering joint to Larry, who took an ample toke and passed it on to Jackie. The party's dim redness had

45

concealed more than dust. In the natural light, Jackie's nose seemed more crooked, and his eyes more irregular, the right socket almost perfectly round, the left almond-shaped. Of course, Jay-Jay's eyes bore the identical distortion, as well as the matching, deep yellow bags underneath. From time to time, Larry had caught bits of bar gossip about the Hellers' incestuous tendencies. He wondered what Barney might be hiding behind his mirrored shades and biker-style scruff, or even Bill with his hippy beard and moustache, and his tinted glasses. The features of Mike and Looey's bare faces appeared balanced, although in Looey's case it was hard to tell because his skin was crawling with pimples.

Bill held the protractor-shaped hand scale before his face and waited for the pointer to reach equilibrium along the measure. He removed a pinch from the sandwich baggie, which was suspended by its backflap from a clip affixed to one end of the scale's beam. The bag looked a hair or two light from Larry's vantage, but Bill unclipped the bag and handed it to Looey, who rolled it up and added it to the quarter-ounce pile on the coffee table.

Larry ground his molars. It wasn't supposed to be like this. He figured they'd want a quarter-pound once every week or two. Instead, this was his second delivery in the seven days since he agreed to supply them, and this delivery was twice the quantity as the first one. Larry had not enjoyed the drive home from Rockford with a half-pound secreted in the Olds' trunk. He guessed he was lucky that so far he'd been a dismal failure as a retail dealer, or pretty soon he'd be transporting full pounds. He was one traffic stop away from a felony charge.

Looey tossed another measured baggy on the pile. Every day at work during the slow stretches Larry had mentally rehearsed the speech he planned to give about how he couldn't score anymore. He surveyed the wide open windows. The cops could show up at any time looking for Slappy. He considered how fast they were selling through their stash. They couldn't be very discriminating when it came to choosing customers. All it took was one moron getting himself busted and the dominoes would fall straight to Larry.

His belly gurgled. His throat was cottonmouth dry. His gaze swept across each individual Heller. Now wasn't the time. But the first chance he had to get Bill alone, then he would do it.

Bill, measuring a fresh bag, looked past the scale at Larry. "With Cheese Days coming, I'm gonna need to bump my order up."

With some effort, Larry focused his eyes on Bill. "Yeah?"

Bill nodded. "I'm thinking two pounds."

Larry swallowed. He ran his tongue around the inside of his mouth. "Kind'a short notice. I don't even know if I can swing that much."

"Shit," Barney said, without turning his head toward Larry, "shouldn't be a problem for a sly motherfucker like yourself."

The twins snickered. Mike shot them a dirty look. Larry figured that by now all the Hellers must have heard about his 'foolproof' pot-dealing scheme. Either that, or they knew about him and Meryl.

Mike cleared his throat and looked at Larry. "We do need to talk about Cheese Days. We need to adjust our deal, just until it's over."

"Adjust it how?"

"You're new around here, so you don't get how crazy it's gonna get. We know the regulars, the carnies, the vendors, people you don't know. People you'd miss. So we're gonna deal in Murray until Cheese Days is over. Afterwards, we go back to the old deal, and Murray's all yours again. Sound good?"

"Fucker don't own Murray," Barney said. "We don't need his permission to do shit."

Mike stared at Barney. "Shut the fuck up. We're doing business here, and if you can't act like a grown up, then get the fuck out."

Barney's lips twitched, but he kept his mouth shut.

Mike held his stare for a second longer, than took a breath and returned to Larry. "Anyways, the more we sell, the more money you make."

Larry wiped a fresh pool of sweat from above his upper lip. "I don't mind."

Mike glanced at Barney while saying, "I knew you'd be reasonable." He scoffed. "Hell, you wouldn't be able to make the rounds anyways because you're gonna be stuck at Bub's the whole time. Shit, between us, and your own customers, and your tips, you'll be making money hand over fist."

Bill chuckled. "Bub's the one who'll be making the real money."

With the back of his hand Jackie tapped Larry on the thigh. "I keep forgetting you work at Bub's. You know that bartender Margaret?

Larry nodded. Mike rolled his eyes.

Jackie smirked. "I fucked that bitch."

Larry noted the exasperated reactions of Mike and Bill. Looey grinned, apparently a true believer. Larry estimated that Jackie was down to his final surviving brain cells, since the burnout didn't seem to remember that he'd claimed the same thing last Saturday night. By the sober light of day, Larry couldn't believe that he'd thought for even a split second that Margaret would let the shirtless marvel touch her.

"For fuck's sake," Mike said. "I'm so fucking sick and tired of you spouting that bullshit. Anyways, everybody knows the real fucking story."

Larry raised an eyebrow. He wanted to hear the real fucking story.

Mike shook his head. "The stupid motherfucker felt her up. She was passed out right here on this couch, and this fucker sneaks in and starts rubbing her titties and her snatch."

Both Bill and Looey broke out laughing.

Mike smiled. "Strictly over the clothes. Fuckin' loser."

Jay-Jay chuckled.

"A couple of her friends walked in on him," Mike said, "caught him with his hands in the cookie jar."

Everybody laughed their asses off, except Barney, who smiled tight-lipped, and Jackie, whose face flushed beet red.

Mike shook, his eyes welling up. "They kicked his ass from here till Sunday! Motherfucker's lucky he didn't go to jail!"

The Hellers howled. Larry laughed too. Even Barney was quaking, showing his brown-stained yellow teeth. Jackie looked like he might start bawling any second. Larry thought it served the little pervert right. If anything, he'd gotten off easy. Just the thought of him groping Margaret made Larry a little hot. A twinge of guilt followed, like he'd felt all week, whenever he saw Margaret and remembered his marathon with Meryl. His guilt was stupid, but he couldn't help it. Meryl had picked up the phone last Monday, when

48

he'd called to make sure Bill would be home the next day to take a delivery, and they'd made awkward chitchat and indefinite plans for the weekend. The day after she'd been elsewhere when he had dropped off the dope. Now it was approaching sundown on Saturday night, and they still hadn't solidified any plans, and he was stoned and feeling all weird about the situation, so … maybe it would be for the best if they kept it to a one-time thing.

Mike and Bill stopped laughing. They looked past Jackie and Jay-Jay. Everybody else stopped laughing. Larry didn't need to look.

Jay-Jay looked over his shoulder. "Hey whirly-Meryly."

Larry tamped down a rueful smile. Think of the Devil …

Meryl sashayed through the space between Larry and Jackie, then plopped down right on Larry's lap. Larry grunted. His heartbeat sped up. He'd imagined a ton of scenarios in which they revealed their tryst to the Heller boys. This was not one of them. Worse, there was nothing even close to innocent about the way she sat on him, with her back to his stomach and her tanned legs inside his, her ass flush on his crotch. They might as well be fucking right in front of her male kin.

But she did smell good. A faint lilac scent drifted from her straight brown hair. The warmth of her soft skin radiated through her thin cut-offs and loose yellow tank top. He sighed. If they didn't know before, they sure did now.

Barney passed her the joint. She took a hit, and still nobody said a word. When she handed the fresh joint to Larry, he was grateful for something other to do than just sit there and burn under their unblinking glares. He leaned behind her to toke, using her body to shield himself. He felt immediate relief, only to stir down below.

Barney, out of the side of his mouth and loud enough for only Meryl and Larry to hear, said, "Man, you just move right in, don'tcha?"

Barney's pissed-off mumbling did nothing to frighten Larry's traitorous, expanding penis. As he finished his hit, Meryl gave him a little wiggle. He exhaled a cloud of smoke, then whispered "You're not helping." She tittered.

Barney growled, "What's so fucking funny?"

Larry ignored him and passed the joint to Jackie, who stared hard at Larry with those crazy eyes. Larry glanced at Mike. He was staring too, but Larry was unable to read his poker face.

Jay-Jay broke the silence, saying to Larry, "Hey Mister Delta 88, why'd you buy such a piece of shit?"

Larry jumped on the opportunity to break the ice. "Ever since I was a kid I loved Oldsmobiles."

"What you got in that heap?" Bill asked.

Larry could've kissed Bill. He talked engines and exhaust systems until his woody went flaccid. Shortly after, Meryl declared that she was bored and suggested that they go for a ride. She grabbed his hand and led him out of the room. He couldn't make out their words from the kitchen, but he was sure that the tone in the living room had turned sullen.

Outside, he said, "So I take it they already knew about us."

She swept her brown bangs behind her ears and smiled. She got into the Olds. When he got in, she said, "Take a left at the end of the lane."

"Where are we going?"

"You'll see."

After he made the turn, she unzipped his pants and pulled his tighty-whities down to his thighs. She began to stroke him. The combination of his mellow buzz and her achingly slow rubbing elevated him into a state of semi-bliss. She gave him directions, and he obeyed. He would have driven off a cliff if she said so. They traveled gravel roads and ended up parked underneath a truss bridge in the middle of nowhere.

Three orgasms later and well after nightfall, they lounged in the backseat. He laid on his back and she nestled into his chest while the sweat cooled on their naked bodies. They shared a cigarette, the only source of light in the pitch darkness under the bridge.

Larry exhaled a stream of smoke. "I don't think your brothers like the idea of me and you."

She expelled a brief hiss. "They're not all my brothers."

"Yeah, so which ones are? I can't keep it straight."

"It's none of their beeswax what I do." She took the cigarette out of his hand and drew a petite puff.

Larry, giving himself points for cleverness, was about to say 'I think they're more worried about who you do.' From behind, on the center of the trunk, a heavy *thump* rocked the Olds.

Larry started and racked his balls on Meryl's knee. He gasped, the breath knocked out of him. More thumps sounded above, and claws skittered on the roof, then across the hood. He felt Meryl sit up and tracked her movements by the cigarette's coal. He craned his neck for a look out the windshield. He felt the Olds wobble as something big launched itself off the roof. Where the pitchy shadow of the bridge gave way to moonlight, squirrels the size of German shepherds streaked into the tall grass.

Agony pulsed up from Larry's testicles. He drew his knees up to his chest and groaned.

"Are you hurt?"

He wheezed, then managed to breathe, "I thought I imagined it. They're real?"

"Yep." She took a drag off the cigarette.

Her lack of surprise provided a slight distraction from his pain. "What, do they follow you around?"

"There's a whole bunch of them out here. They're harmless. I hope they didn't scratch up your paint job."

He blew out a breath and lowered his legs. She found his calves with her free hand and guided them to her lap.

He took the cigarette. "Fucking squirrels." He inhaled a shaky drag. "That reminds me …you wanna hear something weird?" By the time he'd spilled everything about Mrs. Reeves and the squirrel drowning machine his balls had settled into mild discomfort.

She lit another cigarette. After she took a drag he reached for it, but she brushed his hand away. "Why didn't you stop her?"

"Believe me, I've been beating myself up about it ever since."

"You're just gonna let her get away with it?"

He was glad that the darkness covered his blush, but he cringed at his whiney tone as he said, "No. I'm just waiting to catch her in the act."

"You said she did it a week ago."

"I promise I'll put a stop to it."

She leaned over him and eased the cigarette between his lips, then worked her mouth down his torso. Her boobs squashed against him, her hard nipples scuffing down his flesh. She raised her head. "You'd better."

She lowered her head. He moaned, "I will."

Chapter Nine

Larry swatted his neck, smooshing a mosquito against his stubbly skin. The little bloodsuckers sure woke up early. The sun had been singeing the horizon when he'd entered the Weeds. Now, maybe fifteen minutes later, the day was finally brightening to the point where he could tell that the looming shapes were not shadowy fiends with exaggerated claws but rather brown trees and green bushes.

He sat on matted undergrowth and propped his back against a tree in a spot off-trail about twenty yards down from Mrs. Reeves' squirrel-drowning machine. The surrounding chest-high weeds ought to provide all the cover he needed. Wearing boots, jeans, a black long-sleeved tee shirt, and a camouflage-patterned ball cap, he'd overdressed in order to thwart the bugs and the itchweed, but his preparations had the unintended benefit of warming him against the unexpected morning chill. As the nocturnal bugs wound down from a long night of chirruping, and the daytime bugs began to tune up, he found himself at the perfect body temperature for drowsing.

He nodded. His chin touched his chest, then he snapped his head up and harshed in a short breath. He rubbed his eyes. He'd been up all damn night. He should've never told Meryl about Mrs. Reeves and the drowning machine. Meryl just wouldn't let it go, kept bringing it up all the way to when he dropped her off. She'd even cried a little. She'd been so upset that she'd made him too upset to fall asleep. He'd lain awake all night obsessing about what he should do. He kept circling around to the same old plan: hide out and take pictures of Reeves as she worked the machine, then step in at the last second and save the squirrel. But he wasn't in love with the plan. He'd never owned a camera in his life, until last Monday, when he was still hot to confront Mrs. Reeves. He'd bought the cheapest one at Wal-Mart, but now that he was out here, he realized that he hadn't considered the darkness. He had no idea if his photos would turn out, but if they did, he'd make her dismantle the machine and leave the squirrels be, or he'd reveal her insanity to the whole goddamned town.

He swatted another mosquito. Maybe she wouldn't show up. He'd made sure there was a squirrel in one of the traps before he trekked out here, but maybe she had better things to do this Sunday morning, or maybe she'd get one of his fellow borders to release the squirrel in the park. He'd give it ten more minutes. If she didn't show, then fuck it, he needed to crash. He hoped she wouldn't be puttering in the garden when he bumbled out of the Weeds with a camera dangling from his neck. That might be a little hard to explain.

The rattling of the cage on the approaching dolly startled him out of a deeper nod. He sat up. He brought the camera to his face and framed the shot. He had a perfect view of the clearing. The lighting seemed okay.

Mrs. Reeves wheeled the dolly into the clearing. Like a warehouse pro, she slid the blade of the dolly out from underneath the cage. Instead of her usual gardening uniform, she wore dark slacks and a pristine white blouse. Larry guessed she had to be at church extra early. She was wearing her gardening accessories, the brown work gloves, the wide straw hat, and those big black wraparound sunglasses.

While fastening the C-clamp to the cage, her head angled towards Larry. Her thin lips formed a merciless horizontal slash. He was dying to capture her stone-cold expression, but he swallowed, and reminded himself to wait for the burr of the winch-chain to cover the camera's clicks.

A brown blur slammed Reeves out of frame. She screamed. Larry lowered the camera and gaped. He used the tree at his back to boost himself to his feet for a better look.

From the other side of the clearing, they swarmed over her. He counted five monster squirrels, as big as Rottweilers. They flattened Mrs. Reeves on her stomach. She shrieked herself hoarse.

Larry blinked, tried to step back, but bumped into the tree behind him. They tore over her in a darting frenzy, in what seemed at first to be pure feral mayhem, but after a moment, a deliberate pattern emerged: they were scrabbling to pin down her flailing limbs.

One mangy beast straddled her right arm and mashed itself down, its muscular haunches squashing her shoulder, its muzzle at her wrist, its gnawing orange-tinted teeth rending her knuckles.

Broken twigs and shredded leaves poked out of its bushy tail, which curled along its back. Its head turned, and one glossy black eye froze Larry, who sensed deep in his bones that if he didn't move, it wouldn't see him.

A greasy, burnt popcorn stench reached Larry's nose. Reeves screeched "No!" while wrenching her right arm towards her body. The violent shift swept the squirrel's paws out from underneath it and flung it to its flanks. The squirrel rolled upright. It spun around, spraying dirt crumbs, and aimed its head at Reeves. It dashed back into the melee.

Larry broke into a sprint. He mowed through the tall weeds. The popcorn stink made his eyes water. The squirrels, one clinging haphazardly to each limb, held Reeves spread eagle on her belly. A squirrel rode between her shoulder blades, its claws dug into her bloodied and tattered blouse. She kept twisting her head from side to side, thrusting her throat away from the brute's gnawing teeth.

She momentarily overcame her hoarseness and let loose a warbling, soprano-pitched scream. The exertion appeared to sap her strength, and her struggling waned. Larry burst into the clearing. The nearest squirrels sprang away from him, landing on the other side of her body. The beast on her back lifted its blood-matted snout and leveled an inky eye at him.

A furry brown mass thumped into his stomach. He doubled over, then staggered back and dropped to his left knee. Another brown mass of fur, hard muscle and harder bone, smacked into his chest. The knobby blow bent Larry backwards to the dirt, trapping his lower left leg under his hamstring. Larry yipped and rolled away from the sharp pain in his hyperextended knee.

A claw raked Larry under the right eye. He brought up his forearms to protect his face. Teeth closed around his left pinky and he lashed out with his right fist. His punch landed square with an audible *whack*.

Up-trail, a man shouted. Larry recognized the voice of Joe Arnold, one of his housemates. For a moment there was no sound, then Mrs. Reeves' pitiful wail shattered the silence. Larry struggled up to a sitting position. The last of the squirrels bounded over the ledge. Their splashes receded upriver.

Sobs wracked Mrs. Reeves. Her back was a slough of blood and dirt. Her limbs wormed in confused slow-motion. Her wraparound sunglasses lied upside-down in the dirt by her head, with one of their arms snapped off at the hinge.

Larry looked up at Joe Arnold as the burly, middle-aged factory worker entered the clearing. Terry Scheffler, another housemate who was closer to Larry's age and worked as a janitor at the high school, was right behind Joe.

Joe took one look at Mrs. Reeves, then swung into action. He snatched her up and carried her like a baby, hurrying back down the trail.

Terry helped Larry to his feet. After Larry assured Terry that he was all right, Terry looked around the clearing, noting the dolly, the cage – still containing a squirrel – and the chains hanging down from the massive tree. He gave Larry a sidelong stare. "Just what in the Sam Hell were you guys doing down here?"

Larry started toward the cage, gritting his teeth against the pain in his knee, and said, "Ask her."

Chapter Ten

Larry snuffled into a honk, which jolted him back to consciousness, the alcohol stringency of antiseptic surging up nostrils. His eyelids fluttered. The paper hospital gown crinkled against his bare skin, and the examining table's cushions raspberried when he shifted his butt. It seemed like ages ago when he crept out to the Weeds to catch Mrs. Reeves red-handed. The clock over the door indicated less than three hours had passed.

He began to yawn. The door opened and the doctor walked in while he was mid-gape. Her loose lab coat curtained her stout frame. Strands of gray flecked her dark bun. She halted on his left and groped one-handed for the tortoiseshell-framed glasses hanging around her neck while studying his chart.

He covered his mouth with his hand and finished the yawn. "Sorry. God I'm so tired."

"We're just about done." She settled the glasses on the bridge of her nose, then flipped a page on the chart.

"How's Mrs. Reeves?"

"She's shaken up, but nothing serious. We'll keep her overnight, but I think she's going to be fine. She's lucky you were there."

"What about me? Am I gonna make it?"

She chuckled. "Just a sprained knee. The more you stay off it, the quicker it'll heal."

"I'm a bartender."

She nodded. "Ahh. I'll write you a prescription that'll get you through Cheese Days."

"Good."

"There's an officer outside waiting to see you. Are you up to it?"

He nodded. She left the examining room. A few seconds later, the dimple-chinned cop entered. His pink scalp gleamed through his blonde buzzcut. His blue eyes, several shades paler than his navy blue uniform, fixed on Larry. Solid but with a hint of a paunch, he moved easy like an ex-jock, probably played a mean linebacker in high school. He stood about six-two, but the thick heels of his shiny black shoes gave him an extra inch or two of intimidation. The equipment suspended from his utility belt clapped against his body with each step. He had a pocket-sized notebook open in one hand and ballpoint pen in other.

The cop introduced himself as 'Officer Jim.' While scribbling on his notepad, he said, "So you're the hero that saved Mrs. Reeves from a pack of wild dogs."

Larry shook his head. "Not dogs."

Officer Jim sucked his teeth. "Helluva thing. There's been rumors about dog packs out in the country since forever, but I never heard of them coming so far into town before."

Larry raised his voice a notch. "It wasn't dogs. It was bigass squirrels."

Officer Jim looked up from his notepad and scrutinized Larry's eyes. "Just how hard did you get hit in the head?"

"I didn't get hit in the head."

"How much pain medication did Doc give you?"

"None, not yet. Listen, it's the truth. They were humongous squirrels."

Officer Jim peered at Larry. "Who are you?"

"Larry Donaldson ... what do you mean?"

"You're not from around here. I know everybody around here. Is this some kind of Cheese Days stunt?"

"What?"

Officer Jim pointed his pen at Larry. "Don't play dumb with me. Seems like every two years some asshole vendor hears the stories and gets it into his head that he might drum up a little more publicity, get his name in the paper, by pulling some dumb-assed stunt."

"I'm not a vendor. What stories are you talking about?"

"You from the tabloids? We get a couple of you dirtbags sniffing around every once in a while. You know it's a felony to give false information to a police officer."

"I'm not from the tabloids. I swear I'm telling the truth."

Officer Jim raised an eyebrow. "So, you're claiming that Mrs. Reeves is lying."

"Wait ...she said dogs attacked her?"

Officer Jim continued to stare at Larry.

"Maybe she didn't get a good look," Larry said. "Maybe she's in shock. Uh, maybe she thought nobody would believe her." He narrowed his eyes. "Or maybe it was because of what she was doing."

"What was she doing?"

"She kills squirrels. Regular squirrels. She traps them in cages and takes them into the Weeds. She's got a rig set up down there to drop the cages in the river and drown the squirrels."

Officer Jim's upper lip quivered, then he burst out laughing.

Larry scowled. "Go down there and see for yourself. She probably said it was dogs so she wouldn't get into trouble."

Officer Jim wiped the tears from his eyes with the back of his hand. "So you're telling me that giant squirrels attacked her because she was killing regular squirrels? Revenge of the giant squirrels?" He snorted. "Are you on drugs?"

"Just go down and check it out. She's lying because she doesn't want people to find out what she's really been up to."

Officer Jim scoffed. "Why would she care? It ain't illegal to kill squirrels." He scanned the notepad page. "You claim you're not a vendor, not a reporter, so what's your interest in Cheese Days?"

Larry let out a loud exhale. "I'm not here for Cheese Days. I moved to Murray a couple of months ago. I bartend at Bub's. I'm one of Mrs. Reeves' boarders. I don't have anything to do with Cheese Days, I'm not a reporter. I'm just a guy. And by the way, this isn't the first time I've seen them."

"Seen who?"

"The giant squirrels."

"Yeah? When was the first time? "

"At a party, about a week ago."

Office Jim's head waggled as he said, "I've lived around here my whole life and I never saw a trace of them. Where was this party?"

"Mike Heller's place."

Officer Jim craned his nose. "Now it all makes sense. You're a hophead. Were you high when you saw these alleged giant squirrels?"

Larry shook his head. "I wasn't high."

"Look at you. You're eyes are all bloodshot and liddy. What are you on?"

The air-conditioned chill penetrated Larry's paper gown. He tried to suppress a shiver, but a minor tremor quivered through his jaw. "I've been up all night."

"You know we're right here in the hospital. I can have the tests done lickety-split."

Larry bit down on his tongue. A drug test would come back positive for THC. He was certain that Officer Jim wouldn't hear his pleas that pot didn't make you hallucinate. Probably the cop would follow up, find out about his legal issues, and then the judge would rescind his recognizance. He'd spend from now till his next court date in lockup.

Officer Jim stowed his notebook and pen in his shirt pocket. "That's what I thought. Lemme give you a piece of advice. Forget about giant squirrels."

"But they attacked us! Aren't you scared they might hurt somebody else?"

Officer Jim cinched his hands into his utility belt and puffed up his pectoral muscles. "Listen now. The dogcatcher is out searching the Weeds, so don't worry about that. He finds some giant squirrels, then you can personally tell me 'I told you so.' But in the meantime, Mrs. Reeves says it was dogs, so that makes it the word of a God-fearing grandma from a respected family against the word of a hophead from out of town."

Larry sagged.

Officer Jim dipped his dimpled chin and glared at Larry from under his eyebrows. "Right now you're a hero that saved an old lady from a pack of feral dogs. That ain't half bad. But you push it, then we'll have no choice but to go through your business with a fine-toothed comb." He spun on his heel and strode toward the door, which he opened, stepped halfway through, then turned back to Larry and said, "Do the smart thing."

Chapter Eleven

Larry popped a pill. His knee throbbed after working his first scheduled nightshift. He popped another. He decided that he deserved two because he'd pulled a double. It was traditional, or so he'd been told, that on the Thursday before the official start of Cheese Days, Jerry and Matt got the night off. On the bright side, that meant that he'd teamed with Margaret. The shift had zoomed by.

Larry stashed the pill bottle in his jeans and grabbed a damp bar towel. He'd wiped his way around the bartop, with the last foot of lacquered oak to go, when he detected the light scent of cherry-vanilla in the air. As he rotated he figured that Margaret must've given herself a fresh spritz of her tasty perfume.

The candied fragrance blended with her powder-pink tee shirt, its long white sleeves rolled halfway up her forearms, and with her pink canvass Converses, and with her pink fingernails, to create the impression that she was one big treat, her tight faded blue jeans suggesting a pastel wrapper. Her long, loose sandy curls were still bouncy, her green eyes still shiny, even the smattering of freckles across her small nose seemed perky. She brimmed with pep despite the night's brisk trade. Larry, dragging ass, found her just a tad irksome. Until she smiled.

"You coming to the party?"

Larry almost said 'No fucking way.' He cleared his throat. "What party?"

"The Thursday before Cheese Days all the bar and restaurant staff in town gets together after work for the kickoff party. We get to go on the rides for free, the cops look the other way, we party until daybreak. Get it all out of our systems so we can concentrate on work."

Larry scoffed. "It's two in the morning."

"The night is young."

"I should go home and rest my knee. Anyways, I gotta get another rabies shot tomorrow before work."

She tsk-tsked. "Didn't think you'd be such a wuss. For the next ten days everybody gets to have a good time but us. Don't blow your last chance."

He gazed at her. He'd bet anything she didn't lose many arguments. Anyways, he had to know what she meant by 'last chance.' He nodded. "Okay. But just one drink."

He brought the plastic disposable cup to his lips, tipped his head, the mostly-melted ice chips tinkling against his teeth, and he drained his sixth screwdriver.

He lowered the cup and let out an "Ahhh," then watched her make yet another try at the ring-toss game. She underhanded the yellow rubber ring, and it caromed off the center of the set of wine bottles arranged in a triangle, five bottles to a side, on a table about five feet back from the divider. He'd tried to tell her that it was rigged, but she had her heart set on winning a certain stuffed animal, a purple chimp with giant googly eyes.

He laughed at her latest miss. "This is getting out of hand."

She shot him a dirty look. "I'm getting closer."

If she meant that the carny was letting her lean closer with each successive failure, then he had to agree with her. Any closer, and she'd be able to drop the ring right on top of a bottle. He chuckled. He might end up getting less than five hours of sleep before work, but he had to admit that he'd had a good time. They'd gone on every ride, the tilt-a-whirl, the moonwalk, the chair-o-planes, bumper cars, and the carasoul, at least twice, and the Ferris wheel three times. They'd played each game of skill and chance. She had turned out to be a fierce competitor, and a bit of a goofball, claiming that last Cheese Days she'd taken second place in the hotdog eating contest, a claim she passionately defended until he challenged her to a one-on-one match.

He laughed. He couldn't bear to watch her miss again, so he turned his back on her futility and surveyed the carnival. Tents and food kiosks and rides took up the entire city-block-sized parking lot, where square-going shoppers usually parked. The square itself was cordoned off and cheese vendors had filled the courthouse grounds with stalls. The livestock shows, tractor pulls, and the demolition derby, among other activities, would go on at the fairgrounds on the edge of town. Margaret promised him that Cheese Days would be ten days of sheer pandemonium.

He took a deep breath through his nostrils. In this last hour of darkness before dawn, with only half the lights burning and the calliope turned down low, Larry felt like he was straying through a dream. Maybe it was the fatigue, and the booze, and yes, the pills, but everything seemed slowed down and easy. The mellow laughter of old friends. The sparse crowd, insiders only, no waiting in lines. Generous amounts of liquor and food, free to all, yet not so much as a single scuffle, a minor miracle. This was the life.

Margaret punched him in the shoulder. "Check it out."

He contemplated the purple chimp that she thrust an inch away his nose. "I know he gave it to you out of pity."

She scowled.

"He should've," he said. "You only spent about twice what that thing is worth."

She shoved the chimp into his hands. "Come on, let's go get a nightcap."

He carried the chimp while she led him to a bank of trailers, the temporary homes of the carnies. He followed her up a set of homemade wooden steps and through the wide open front door of a trailer.

A narrow kitchenette bordered one end of the living room, and a wall bisected by a darkened hallway bordered the other. A lava lamp illuminated the room with a gooey yellow glow. Four people squeezed onto one couch, five on the other, and everybody else sat on the floor or stood in small groups. The majority wore long hair and blue jeans and rock-concert tee shirts, and it seemed like everybody was smoking something, the atmosphere near the ceiling thickening to a tobacco and marijuana haze.

A massive dude with a shaved head, standing right inside the door, tapped Margaret on the shoulder. She looked at the guy then let out a little squeal. She gave him a big hug. Larry had never seen the guy before. Margaret fell into an animated conversation with the guy. Larry couldn't hear what they were saying over the general chatter in the room. He felt a twinge of jealousy. He lit a cigarette. Guys had been greeting Margaret all night long, and she knew most of their names. She was just a friendly girl, that's all. Something he told himself he'd better keep in mind, before he got too carried away.

Larry turned away from them and spotted a couple of familiar, hairy faces. Bill and Slappy were already making their way toward him. Larry groaned. He knew he couldn't retreat. He figured his only move was to meet them halfway and hope that the crowd blocked Margaret from seeing, and from approaching before he could blow them off, before they let it slip to her that he was their pot supplier, or worse, that he'd screwed Meryl.

Larry shouldered through clusters and tried to veer out of Margaret's eyeline. As soon as they were finished with their hellos, Slappy handed Larry a smoking joint. Margaret chose that moment to step up to Larry's other side. Larry looked at her, looked at the joint, looked at her again.

She snatched the joint out of his hand. With her free hand, she poked him in the chest. "If you tell anyone I'll murder you."

He leaned back, then a nervous chuckle escaped his lips. She laughed, then took a respectable hit. Larry glanced at Bill, whose blank expression felt like a punch to the guts. Larry hadn't thought about Meryl at all for at least the last twelve hours. He shifted his eyes toward Slappy, who had a silly, stoned-out-of-his-mind grin on his face, and he felt a little calmer.

Margaret handed the joint to Larry and took her purple chimp back. Larry drew a deep drag off the joint and gave it to Slappy. After Larry exhaled, he said to Margaret, "You know Bill?"

Margaret smirked. "Everybody knows these guys."

Slappy looked at his shoes. Bill said, "Everybody knows Margaret, too."

They passed the joint one more time around, then Margaret grabbed Larry's elbow and said, "Let's get some fresh air."

Larry let her pull him along, giving the Hellers a sheepish wave. Once outside, he drew a deep breath. He was happy to be free of the smoggy trailer, but even happier to get away from Bill's steady gaze.

"I think it's time to call it a night," Margaret said.

"I think you're right."

"We'd better walk home."

"But my car ..."

"Will be where you left it. C'mon, my place isn't far from here. And your place is just a stone's throw from mine."

They started off at a slow stroll. He felt an intense urge to hold her hand. He wondered if she'd let him if he tried. His sluggish brain lurched ahead, and he said, "You know where I live?"

"It's a small town, people talk." She shot him a coy head-tilt. "After all, you are the mysterious new stranger in town."

"People talk about me?"

"Shhhh. People are sleeping."

Man he was wasted. He hadn't even noticed they were already in a residential neighborhood. Now that she'd brought it to his attention, even their footsteps seemed loud in the pre-dawn tranquility.

In a lower tone, he said, "People talk about me?"

"All the girls think you're handsome."

He grinned. "Oh yeah? What do you think?"

She shrugged. "You're not totally gross."

He laughed. "Thanks. Thanks a lot."

She hushed him again, then said, "Mostly people wonder why you moved to town."

He chewed his tongue. "It's complicated."

"Ahh, so there's a woman involved."

He slid his hands into his pockets.

A couple of paces later, she said, "No pressure, tell me when you want to. *If* you want to."

He sighed. "Thanks." He almost said, 'If I was gonna tell anybody, it would be you,' but then he thought he'd be sticking his neck out too far. And where would it end? He'd tell her about what Deanne did to him, and then he'd have to confess about the dealing, and then about Meryl, and then she'd run away from his dumb ass as fast as she could.

They walked about a block in silence, then she said, "So how do you know the Hellers?"

"I met Slappy at the bar. He invited me out to a party. It was quite an experience." His cheeks flushed. Technically, he hadn't lied …

"It's been a while since I've gone to one of their parties."

"I don't doubt it."

64

"Oh, you heard about that? Is that pervert still saying he got into my pants?"

He nodded.

"That little creep. If I had a dime for every guy who says he scored with me, I could retire. You know the true story?"

He chuckled. "Yep. Should've pressed charges against him."

"I should have."

Her shoulder brushed his, on purpose, it seemed to him. Too soon, she stopped in front of a walkway and said, "This is me."

He observed the small, two-story white house. Flowerbeds bordered the porch and the walk. The grass was tallish but even. A birdbath stood in the left section of the lawn. "Wow, you're a homeowner."

"Used to be my parent's place. Now it's all mine."

"Huh." He continued to regard the house while he considered his next move.

She kissed him on the mouth before he was ready. She was down the walk before he knew what happened. Partway through her front door, she turned and called, "Good night," and then she was gone.

He stood dazed for a moment, then he spun to his left. He looked down the street, realized he'd turned the wrong way, and he pivoted and started back. He hoped she hadn't been watching.

A couple of blocks fuzzed by while he puzzled through what just happened. A friendly peck? Those landed on cheeks, not lips. But she'd been far from sober. People did stupid things when they were drunk, stupid things they regretted the day after. But on the other hand, booze loosened people up, made them do what they really wanted to do. He exhaled, and scolded himself for analyzing it to death. She'd kissed him. He could see them in that little white house, spooning on the couch, maybe a couple years down the line a little boy and a little girl horsing around on the front lawn …

A disturbance above snapped him back to the outside world. On instinct he raised his forearms to protect his head while skipping to the side. He looked up at the dark green canopy. The soft light of streetlamps could not penetrate the dense leafage. The breeze soughed through the gently rocking branches, but the wind was nowhere near strong enough to account for the violent commotion that had startled him out of his thoughts. Or maybe he imagined it. He *was* totally wrecked.

He continued to search the treetops. All was calm, the only movement was the sleepy sway of branches, the only sound the rasp of leaves rubbing against one another. He looked homewards. Three and a half blocks, trees lining the street the whole way, their boughs close to spanning the narrow cross streets of the sylvan neighborhood.

A crackle drew his eyes toward a swinging branch, which dipped downward, and he spotted a dark shape among the shadowy green, a dark shape massive enough to be a giant squirrel. The branch rebounded upward, and he lost sight of the dark shape in the canopy.

He didn't wait for the branch to dip again to be sure. He ran.

Two strides in, the pain in his knee blasted through the buffers of the various pain killers circulating in his system. He grimaced and ran as fast as his limp allowed. Over the slaps of his footfalls he was certain that he heard giant squirrels crashing through the foliage above him. Sounded like a pack of them leaping from branch to branch, striving to outpace him so they could come bombing down from the trees right on top of him.

His abused lungs began to fail him. He coughed as he ran, the phlegmy explosions so loud in his ears that he couldn't hear anything else. He labored to his block, knowing that if they chose to attack, he'd be too exhausted to defend himself. He swerved into the neighbor's lawn and raged at himself for not thinking of this tactic sooner. He scrambled up his front porch and gasping, he wheeled around.

There was no sign of them. He checked all the nearby treetops as he took deep breaths. Nothing. Just the usual, gentle sway. He whispered, "God damn it."

He pulled out his pack of Marbs and shook one out. Tremors pulsed through his hand. He stared at the cigarette and willed the tremors to stop. A series of coughs wracked his lungs and throat. When the fit passed, he looked over the trees. So many trees. And so dense. They had his scent now. His stomach roiled. He slid the cigarette back in the pack and hurried inside, locking the door behind him.

Chapter Twelve

Larry caught himself humming. He couldn't squelch the bounce in his step. Three nights in a row. This time, he'd made out with Margaret until he couldn't stand it anymore. This time, they'd both been sober. She said that she couldn't trust herself if she invited him inside. It had taken two blocks just to walk his boner down to half-mast. A few more blocks to go, and then he'd probably lie awake the rest of the night mooning over her.

He'd almost bit the bullet and told her about the whole mess with Deanne. He knew he had to tell her. No matter how much he wanted to believe that somehow he'd managed to fly under the radar, sooner or later somebody was gonna recognize him, and it'd be a million times worse if somebody else blabbed his disgrace to her.

He stopped in his tracks. Ahead, in the middle of the next block, a dark zone obstructed his route. An especially dense section of canopy swallowed a dead streetlamp. Underneath, the sidewalk stretched darker for about twenty yards.

He scoffed. On *that* night, he'd been sleep-deprived and high on pot, booze, pain medication, and most of all, Margaret. On that night, his addled brain had been wide open to paranoia. Now this. His immediate suspicion was ridiculous. Squirrels didn't set traps. *Don't be chicken.* He resumed his normal gait.

As he neared the dark patch, glass shards glinted on the sidewalk. He squinted upward. The leaves obscured the streetlamp's head, but he was a bartender and he knew damn well what a broken bottle looked like. And Murray's persnickety homeowners did not tolerate littered sidewalks. He didn't have to be Sherlock Holmes to deduce that somebody had smashed the light out, recently.

He stopped. He performed a slow exhale. Just kids throwing rocks. A coincidence. People are too busy to sweep the sidewalk in front of their house. Town Maintenance was way too busy keeping the square clean to bother with providing the usual residential services. Anyways, how in the heck could a squirrel, no matter how big, bust out one of those heavy-duty lamp covers? Plus, if he went around, then he might as well check himself into the nuthouse. He figured that something like the conviction that giant squirrels were after him would gnaw away at his sanity until he woke up one day with full-blown dementia.

Eyes focused on the treetops, he stepped into the darkness. A dozen breathless strides, then he crunched glass under his boots. A chunk lodged into the outer sole of his left boot, adding an odd click to his step. He stopped and tapped the toe of his left boot against the sidewalk until the glass loosened and fell. Now there was no sound but his light footfalls and the breeze through the trees.

He remembered to breathe, and resumed walking. He kept both his eyes and ears peeled. A step away from the light, an overhead rustle caused him to wheel and scan the branches.

He whispered, "Come on you son of a bitches."

The quiet treetops showed no hint of giant squirrels. He grunted, then backed away, his eyes fixated on the shadowy branches. Once out of the darkness, he gave the treetops one more hard look, then about-faced. As soon as he did, leaves swished from behind.

He spun. He located the swaying of branches, and he marked the dim, giant squirrel-sized shape perched among the foliage above.

"I see you." He stepped back with his right foot and shifted so that he led with his left shoulder. He bent his knees slightly and raised his fists up to chin level, his elbows covering his midriff. His muscles remembered the fighting stance he'd learned a few years ago during a sixteen-month stint as student of karate.

The squirrel's silhouette bobbed on the overweighted branch. Larry's heartbeat pulsed sharp and fast. He tucked his jaw and reminded himself to breathe. A wrecking ball-like mass bashed into his lower back.

The shocking blow forced his back to arch until his spine reached the limits of its flexibility before driving him forward. The slightly raised edge of a sidewalk square caught the toe of his boot. He stumbled, then went down hard on his knees.

A furry mass slammed onto the top of his head and left shoulder, kinking his neck to his right shoulder. He fell crooked, to the right side of the sidewalk, thumping into the grass.

He pushed himself up to his hands and knees. Claws shredded his shirt and then his skin before he was able to buck the creature off.

He scrambled around but they wouldn't let him get to his feet. Teeth and claws ripped into his forearms as he shielded his face. They growled through his skin and shirt, which were clamped between their teeth. He heaved himself backward and up to his feet, tearing away from them, the effort blurring his vision.

He saw two, maybe three giant squirrels. One darted toward him and he lashed out with his boot. He connected somewhere around the thing's belly, and it gave out a surprised squeak as the strike changed the squirrel's trajectory. It thudded to the sidewalk, whomping onto its side.

Larry charged the remaining squirrels. His sudden surge made his head spin. One smacked into the back of his left calf, buckling him back down on his knees in the grass. Another battered into his stomach, knocking the wind out of him. He retched. He threw a blind punch, and he snarled when it connected with flesh and bone. He flopped to his belly, rolled to his side, and passed out.

He heard his own voice repeating, while accelerating to a crescendo, "I'm dying, I'm dying, I'm dying …"

He shot up into a sitting position. Giant squirrels sprang away from him. The squirrels whirled to face him, their paws splayed, their muzzles low to ground, their tails curling into the air. He touched his neck in the neighborhood of his jugular and his hand came away bloody.

Adrenaline rippled through him. He lunged at the squirrels. They bolted, scattering in different directions. He twisted upward and got his feet underneath himself.

He slurred, "No," as he swooned, his field of vision dissolving to black.

Chapter Thirteen

Officer Jim looked up from his notepad. "Can you give me a description of the punks that assaulted you?"

Larry scowled. From the reclined vantage of his hospital bed, he thought Officer Jim's buzzcut looked a touch shaggy. Purplish circles smudged the skin under his pale blue eyes. Patchy stubble sprouted across his checks, a dark swathe filling in his chin dimple. Sweat darkened the armpits of his navy blue uniform. Larry supposed that because of the workload of policing the festival, Officer Jim no longer had the time for regular shaves and haircuts, or even a good night's sleep. His shoulders and jaw kept slumping, until he noticed his slack posture, and then he'd snap his mouth shut and thrust out his broad chest while straightening his spine.

Larry brushed away the stirrings of pity, instead focusing on the cop's willful ignorance. "Look at me!" He raised his bandaged arms and pointed at the white brace wrapped around his neck. "My back's all clawed up, they gnawed on my arms and my neck … Jesus Christ, man!"

Officer Jim's brow wrinkled. He began jotting notes on his pad. "Bruises about the head, neck, chest, and stomach. Skinned knees, elbows, and knuckles. Injuries consistent with a fistfight." He stopped writing and gazed at Larry. "The citizen that found you laying in his front yard claimed he heard a car peel out a few blocks away."

Larry shook his head. "It was giant squirrels."

Officer Jim's eyelids dropped halfway. "How high were you at the time of the assault?"

"Nuh-uh. I was stone cold sober. They're out to get me."

Officer Jim rubbed his forehead.

"Ever since Cheese Week started," Larry said, "they've been stalking me."

"Cheese Days."

Larry let his sudden spike of heat subside, then said, "I hear them following me, when I'm walking home, up in the trees …do I need to catch one to prove it to you?"

Officer Jim flipped his notepad shut. "I think we're done here."

"Listen. They want to kill me because I saved Mrs. Reeves. They wanted to kill her."

Officer Jim chuckled. "I'm sorry, I know it's wrong to laugh, but goddamn, boy! Do you hear yourself?

"I know it sounds crazy. But it's the truth, and … and you *know* it."

Officer Jim's smile dissolved. He lowered his head. "I asked Doc. Hallucinations are one of the possible side affects of your medication. Add booze and pot, and who knows what else, and all bets are off."

"No. I know what I saw."

Officer Jim pocketed his notepad and crossed his arms over his chest. "I know you're in cahoots with the Hellers."

Larry spun his wheels before blurting, "What?"

"Don't bother denying it. We got witnesses that put you with them."

Larry stammered. He couldn't think of anything to say.

Officer Jim nodded. "Yep. And all of a sudden, there's pot all over the goddamned place. Every two-bit scumbag who gets busted, or gets pulled over, or for whatever reason comes to our attention, seems to have a little bag of weed on his person. Town's dry for ages, then you show up, hook up with the Hellers, and then the town's flooded. One plus one equals two."

Larry rasped, "No."

"One of the good things about living in a small town is that the bad guys can't hide amongst the other bad guys. You stick out like a sore thumb. Makes detective work a helluva lot easier."

Larry bit his tongue. He warned himself to keep his mouth shut.

Officer Jim beamed. "But that don't mean I'm lazy. I found out all about you."

Larry tasted bitter acid in the back of his mouth.

Officer Jim leaned forward, and, hushing his voice, said, "Here's the deal. As soon as you can get out of this bed, you hit the fucking road. Otherwise, I open my big fat mouth."

"You … you can't do this."

Officer Jim straightened. "Yeah, yeah, maybe I'm being too much of a hardass. Anyways, it's only a matter of time till we bust you. So lemme tell ya what. I'll keep quiet for a couple of days. After that, you're still around, then I spread the word about why you came to town in the first place." He sniffed, then said, "You have yourself a nice day."

Chapter Fourteen

The end credits began to roll. Margaret squeezed Larry's hand, their fingers interlocked, his right arm cradling her warm body, which spooned inside his. He inhaled the clean fragrance of her hair. He could lie on her couch like this forever. Word of the attack had apparently spread all over town in a matter of hours. She'd phoned him from work to insist that he come over after her shift so that she could nurse him. Maybe it was only pity that prompted her to finally let him inside her house, but he'd take it.

Emanating from the lower section of a fancy lamp, the low orange glow gleamed across the polished end table by his head. A hanging garden of shoots and vines cascaded down the multi-tiered plant stand running the length of the picture window, the window's deep curtain drawn tight against prying eyes. Knickknacks, framed photos, and books adorned the shelves of the entertainment unit that housed the TV. An afghan, folded into a neat square, draped over the back of the comfy chair catercorner to their feet. Their combined weight sank into the couch's plush cushions.

She gave his hand another squeeze. He tightened his clutch. She'd cranked up the air conditioner, the cool making the blanket covering their bodies a necessity. So far, he'd managed to keep from boning up and spoiling the tender mood, but when she shifted, and his arm grazed her boobs, or her fine ass pressed into his crotch, he'd had to take extreme measures to divert his mind from sex. He caught himself smiling. *All in good time.* He could see himself lying with her in this room for the rest of his life.

She disentangled herself and sat up. He groaned. She twisted toward him. "Did I hurt you?"

His spine crackled as he stretched. His knee felt a little balky. "I feel fine. Good pills." She bounded up. He reached for her, moaning, "Come back."

She ejected the tape from the VCR and stowed it in the rental case. Dishevelment made her long sandy curls look kind'a sexy. Her threadbare powder-blue tee shirt rode up a bit and exposed a tantalizing peek of bare back. The hiked-up left leg of her gray sweats displayed a smooth, slender calf above her blue socks.

Bending to switch off the TV, she said, "You can hardly keep your eyes open. You need your rest if you're gonna make it through your shift tomorrow."

He enjoyed the view for a moment, then said, "I'll be fine. Can't miss a day during Cheesy Days anyways."

She circled back around the low glass coffee table and stood over him. "Playing the tough guy, eh?" She let him pull her down so that she sat sideways in the space in front of his crotch, but she fended off his tentative caress and performed a gentle straightarm to keep him from pulling her back down into spooning. She touched the bandage under his eye. "First dogs, now this? You're one unlucky fella."

A pang flared in his guts, but he couldn't tell her the truth. He feigned a bit of swagger, grousing, "It took a bunch of them to take me down."

"Maybe you shouldn't walk home at night until Cheese Days is over."

With a dismissive hand wave, he snorted. "They caught me off guard." He pitched his voice sarcastic while saying, "Anyways, I got nothing to worry about. Officer Jim's on the case."

She clasped her hands in her lap. She shook her head, a little smile on her face, and she uttered a bemused, "Tsss." A faraway look drifted into her eyes. "That James …"

His chest constricted. He realized he didn't know anything about her. She and 'James' could've been high school sweethearts, could've been prom queen and king, for all he knew. His tongue seemed thick and too big, when he said, "You two had a thing?"

She smirked. "I'm sure you're no angel."

The things he did to Meryl riffled through his mind, then crashed into the image of Deanne, and the cameras, and the host reading the results of the paternity test …

She leaned away and smiled down on him. "I mean, you've hardly told me anything about yourself."

He managed to return her expectant gaze, but the couch beneath him seemed to teeter. He hadn't seen or talked to Meryl since that night under the bridge. Neither of them had said word one about dating. He *should* tell her about Deanne and that whole mess, but now it didn't really matter because the big confession was that her apparent ex-boyfriend had warned him that very morning to get

74

hell out of Dodge. But if he told, he'd have to tell her why, he'd have to tell about the dealing, and about the giant squirrels, and by that time, Deanne, Meryl, that'd just be overkill.

He resisted the urge to lick his dry lips. "Not much to tell." He regretted the pills, they made his aches go away, but they made it hard to think, too. He could tell her about Deanne, and then 'James,' could say whatever the hell he wanted to say. He could quit dealing, and then he wouldn't have to worry about the cops at all. But she wasn't the kind of girl who would go for a drug dealer. If she found out later, well, she was definitely the kind of girl who would dump a liar. And if he told her that giant squirrels were stalking him …

She turned her back to him. She bent, rolling her sock up and working her sweatpants' leg back down. "I'm beginning to think you're hiding something from me."

He held his breath. This was it, she was practically inviting him to spill his guts. A few heartbeats flitted by, then he said, "I don't know hardly anything about you either."

"Yeah, but you're the mysterious stranger in town." Her voice smaller, she said, "I'm sick and tired of getting burned."

"I won't burn ya, I'm cool, baby." He tried to draw her near, but she brushed off his hands. He felt sick to his stomach. His attempt to lighten the mood appeared to be a big mistake.

She leaned toward him, locking in eye contact, and massaged his shoulder. "I think we should keep things between us on the back burner until Cheese Days is over, when we have time to take a deep breath and figure it all out. All right?"

He fought hard to keep the bitterness from contorting his lips. He cursed himself for being a fool. He nodded.

She said, "Time for bed." She tucked him in, then gave him a goodnight kiss on the lips, the kiss lingering long enough to confuse him. She left him and switched off the lamp. The closing of her door cut off her bedroom's light and total darkness enveloped him. He shivered and pulled the covers up to his chin. He was stupid to think that a woman like her would fall for a loser like him. He'd only gotten this far because, as she said, she didn't know anything about him. The cops were after him. Giant squirrels were after him. He had no good reason to stick around.

Chapter Fifteen

Larry limped out of the house and down the steps of the front porch. His left knee was killing him, his right knee only torturing him. He hurt all over, but he couldn't chance taking pills right now. He carried a black duffel bag in his left hand.

He paused on the walkway. The sun shined on the usual cars and trucks parked up and down the street. In the distance, the carnival babbled right through the dinnertime hour. His head wilted. He resumed limping.

He stowed the duffel bag in the Olds' trunk. He lowered himself into the driver's seat and took off. At the town's limit, he reclined from his rigid hunch, sighed, and took a last look in the rearview. A patrol car trailed three blocks behind him. He gave the Olds a little gas. He paid strict obedience to every rule of the road.

About a mile out of town he turned off the highway and onto a gravel road that slashed a dusty yellow through the green ocean of corn. Another mile or so he saw a possum near the shoulder of his side of the road. He swerved wide as the possum waddled into the grassy ditch.

Behind him, the patrol car's cherries strobed. Larry pulled over. The cop coasted to a stop a couple car lengths behind him. Larry adjusted his rearview. Officer Jim sat behind the patrol car's wheel.

Larry fidgeted his fingers on the steering wheel. Finally, a couple of county boys, approaching from the opposite direction, parked in front of Larry, the first Crown Vic almost nose to nose with the Olds.

Officer Jim got out of his car and sauntered up to Larry's door. The county boys got out too, but they hung back, letting Officer Jim take the lead. Office Jim smirked down at Larry. "Hellers live out this way."

"I guess so."

"You ain't so smart, are ya?"

"I'm just trying to leave town, like you told me."

"Allright," Officer Jim said. "Get out of the vehicle."

Between Officer Jim and the stone-faced county boys, they put him through about two dozen sobriety tests, including touching his nose with the tips of his finger and walking a straight line, all, he knew, in the quest for probable cause. Under normal circumstances, he might've acted a little more cocky with each small victory, but with his catalogue of injuries, each test was a major bitch. When they'd exhausted their bag of tricks, Officer Jim waved the county boys over to Larry. "Take a whiff."

One of the brown-shirted cops leaned towards Larry and sniffed. "Yeah, I smell it."

"You smell like cannabis," Officer Jim said. "We're gonna have to search your vehicle."

Larry bit his lower lip. He guessed they hadn't pulled this particular stunt in the first place only because they wanted to torment him. "No way this holds up in court."

They scoured the front and back seats without finding so much as an old beer can. Then they made a big show of popping the trunk. Larry studied Officer Jim's face, which, in the time it took to unzip a duffel bag, flashed from eager anticipation to bafflement, then from bafflement to utter embarrassment. Larry bit back a smile.

The cops huddled for a moment, then broke up. The county boys returned to their cruisers, Officer Jim dogging them as far as their doors, whispering furiously all the while. The county boys sped off, their tires kicking up gravel.

Larry walked to the Olds' trunk, which the cops had left open. His clothes, which he'd packed neatly into the duffel bag, were scattered around the inside of the trunk. His spare tire and jack lied in the gravel. He started shoving tee shirts back into the bag.

Officer Jim stomped up. "You think you're pretty damned smart, don'tcha?"

Larry tilted his head downward in the attempt to hide the grin that he couldn't keep from his lips. "I don't know what you're talking about, Officer."

"The clock's still ticking."

Larry swallowed his glee. He met Officer Jim's pale blue glower and managed an earnest tone, saying, "I'd hate to leave Bub in the lurch. Why don't you give me till the end of Cheese Days?"

Officer Jim, his cheeks blotchy red, said, "No. Ya got till sundown tomorrow. I'll tell Margo personally."

Larry glared, hating to think she'd ever be with a goon like this.

"Yeah," Officer Jim sneered. "I know all about that. I'll tell her about your little game with the Hellers, too. She'll hate your fucking guts."

As Officer Jim strolled away, he called over his shoulder, "Have a nice day."

Larry flung the duffel bag into the trunk. He muttered, "*Asshole.*"

Chapter Sixteen

The last rays of the setting sun lost their grip on the Weeds. The greens and browns blackened, the shadows deepened and lengthened. Larry wrung the bat's handle, his clammy palms slipping on the threadbare tape. He chose a spot under the most porous section of canopy he could find, but the trees loomed so thick, and the night swooped in so fast, that the treetops disfigured into a dark weave of branches and leaves, offering plenty of sturdy perches perfect for ambushing squirrels.

He grazed the polished wood across his cheek, its nicks and dents scraping his skin. He'd found the antique bat in the garage. The heft of its barrel against his jawbone slowed his pulse. Nightbirds twittered. Bugs chirruped, but so far his thorough application of insect repellent kept the biters at bay. A chemical vapor rose from his tee shirt and sweaty skin and invaded his mouth, where the astringency infused the bitterness sludging up his gullet. He performed a faint hock and spit, gaining a momentary respite before the bitterness slimed upward again.

Upriver, a splash froze him. He blinked, re-gripped the bat, and waggled it by his ear. His pounding heartbeat drowned out the night sounds. His eyes darted toward the treetops, then back towards the river. They would attack from above, they were sure to attack from above … but last night, their trap fooled him … they'd want him to think they were attacking from above.

Bushes ruffled, a ways off to the front. He shifted sideways to the sneaky sound. They'd made a mistake. He peered, searching for motion in the darkness. A twig snapped, closer. He cocked the bat by his ear. He knew they'd be watching, waiting for another shot at him. He dropped into a slugger's crouch. Pings from his knees began to puncture his pain killers' buffers. His sore shoulders quivered. The bat seemed ten times heavier.

A dark shape moved. He squinted. Shadows could play tricks on the eyes. A swiping through weeds preceded dark shapes, two, maybe three, riffling over the paler gloom between tree trunks, down near the undergrowth. Larry made a conscious effort to bare his teeth, but stopped when they started to chatter. A crackle sounded closer than seemed possible, close enough that a hurtling charge might beat the swing of his bat. He stepped back, his butt bumping a tree trunk.

"*Pssst!*"

A tiny yelp spurted out of Larry. He swung the bat, which whiffed through the air. He cranked into an awkward, left-handed return cut that hit nothing. "*Larry!*" A line of drool gushed out of his mouth. He raked the back of his hand across his lips, then breathed out a shuddery, "Jesus Christ."

The stalking noises clarified to the sound of sneakers and boots tromping underbrush down to the dirt. Larry took a deep gathering breath, but his voice still came out shaky when he said, "Over here."

He lowered the bat as a pair of humans emerged from the shadows. The mingled scents of marijuana and cigarettes reached his nostrils. The hippy beard and tinted glasses marked the leader as Bill. The follower said, "Hey man," and Slappy's friendly tone jibed with his long, stringy hair and short stature, which was a notch below Bill's.

"What's up?" Bill said. "Why'dja wanna meet here?"

Slappy stepped forward and locked Larry into a fumbling handshake. Larry said, "Where's Mike?"

"He's taking care of some shit," Bill said.

Slappy mumbled something.

Larry faced Bill. "Did you bring the money?"

"What money? Jay-Jay said you called, wanted to meet me in the Weeds."

"*Damn it.*" He squeezed the bat's handle. "The cops are after me. I gotta get out of town by tomorrow night."

"What?" Slappy said. "You can't take off, man!"

"I got to. You know Officer Jim? He gave me till tomorrow night."

"Officer Asshole," Bill said.

"Yeah, well, he figured it out," Larry said. "I wanted to front what I have left to you, and collect whatever I could. I need cash to set up somewhere else."

Bill shrugged. "Sorry man, I didn't know. I don't have that much anyways."

"I thought you were selling like crazy."

80

"We are. But Mike came up with a special angle for Cheese Days."

Larry pursed his lips.

"See," Bill said, "dudes wanna get stoned all during the festival, but they don't got much spare scratch, 'cause they're spending like crazy, you know, their girls, their kids, whatever. Mike was afraid we'd miss out, so he decided we'd front to dudes, and they don't have to pay up until after Cheese Days, but it costs them a little extra. We wait a little bit longer, but we get a lot more, you know, charge interest like on a loan."

Larry stared at the ground, then sighed. "I guess we'll have to work out some way for me to collect. I guess I can live in my car for a while."

Slappy stood on his tiptoes, but still fell far short of meeting Larry eye to eye. "I bet Mike'd let you stay at the house. I know Meryl'd like to see ya."

Larry scrunched his head lower. He gave thanks that the darkness covered his red-hot face. He supposed he'd better make up a lie asserting that he hadn't forgotten about her. He couldn't speak the truth, that the only time he'd thought about her was when he tried to figure out a way to explain things to Margaret.

Bill *scritched* his beard. "I don't know, we kind'a got a full house right now."

Slappy muttered, "Plenty of room back by the barns ..."

"Anyways," Bill said, "that don't solve the problem."

Slappy leaned toward Larry, then said, "What happened to your eye, man?"

Larry touched the scar above his cheekbone. "Oh, nothing. Just a little tussle. Job hazard, ya know."

Slappy frowned. "Why ya got a baseball bat?"

Larry let out a nervous scoff, then swept the bat's tip through some low weeds. "Use it to clear a path."

"Lemme talk to Mike," Bill said. "We might have a move here, but I'll need'ja to stick around until the day after tomorrow."

"What can you guys do?"

"We've lived around here since forever," Bill said. "Don't worry, that asshole won't be parked outside your door with a stopwatch. He'll be too busy policing the festival. Park your car in the garage or something."

"I don't know."

"Even if we can't get you a little breathing room, it'll at least give me some time to collect some cash, give you a little to get started on."

Larry massaged his bicep. He wanted to believe Bill. Maybe it wasn't too late to come clean to Margaret, maybe if he said it the right way she'd be able to get past it all. He supposed he really didn't have anything to lose. He nodded.

"Cool!" Slappy said. "Hey, you wanna catch one?"

Larry smiled in spite of himself. Then he scanned the treetops. "No, I'd better get going."

Slappy huffed. Bill, already stepping away, said, "Sit tight. We'll be in touch."

Chapter Seventeen

Larry held the pub's door for Margaret. She breezed by him, a loose ponytail hiking her sandy curls off of her shoulders, her boobs emphasizing the Chicago Cubs logo on her gray tee shirt, her ass frisky under her tight faded jeans, even though she just finished another festival-intensified shift. He chided himself for ogling. He had to stay focused. He was gonna tell her everything. Her response would determine if he was gonna stick around.

His slight limp slowed his catching up to her brisk stride. She dug her hands into her jean's front pockets. Across the stall-crammed courthouse grounds, weary vendors drudged through the final steps of closing routines. Drunks, in groups small but loud, loitered outside of shuttered bars

Larry's gaze scanned to the right, up the intersecting street, catching flickers of sidewalk-occupying revelers through the cracks between the crush of tall booths and broad, squat counters. He glimpsed messy long hair framing mirrored shades. *Barney*. Larry stared at the far corner of the intersecting sidewalk. Behind Barney, jean shorts cut off and frayed above the knee, shirtless, Jackie swaggered, his twin Jay-Jay behind him. Larry searched the sporadic view for the others. A brawny dude, his brown moptop much shorter than Barney and the twins' tangled manes, but standing head and shoulders above and twice as wide, strolled along the sidewalk in Margaret and Larry's direction. He led the gang of stunted Hellers through the gaps that all the sidewalk drunks ceded to him.

"Oh great," Margaret said.

Larry saw that she'd spotted the Hellers too. "Who's the big guy?"

"Casey Heller. He shouldn't be out of prison this soon."

The Hellers dallied by a storefront, lit cigarettes, studied the sky, but at least one of them seemed to glance this way the whole time. Larry'd bet anything they were pissed about how he treated Meryl. It must look like he banged her and blew her off when something better came along. He had to make things right with Meryl, one more thing he had to do to make things right with Margaret.

"Now they're gonna be even worse," Margaret said.

"What'd he do?"

"I'm not a hundred percent sure, but I know he beat up a cop pretty bad. He was supposed to be gone for years. Everybody in town was happy about that. Since he's been gone, there hasn't been anywhere near the trouble there used to be."

Great. Larry could laugh off Barney, but he couldn't see anything funny about that prison-hardened brute thinking that Larry had wham-bam-thankya-ma'ammed his little sister or cousin or whatever Meryl was to him. The way the Hellers were acting looked like stalling, like waiting to trail him into the darker neighborhoods. "What kind of trouble?"

"Fights, mostly, but he thinks he's God's gift to women, too."

"Did you date him?"

"God no!" She scoffed, then said, "You must think I'm a slut!"

"No, no, no." A row of stalls seemed to engross the Heller Boys, even as they drifted closer.

"He's hit on me before, but I would never ... I do know a few girls who say he won't take 'no' for an answer."

"You mean rape?"

She sighed. "Let's just say that not many women around here are stupid enough to end up alone with him anymore."

A brief flash of red lights drew Larry's attention away from the Hellers. A patrol car parked in front of the wooden barricades cordoning off the square. A pair of cops got out and walked toward the Hellers. Casey puffed up his chest, his torso thrusting out of the flaps of his unbuttoned blue denim vest. A semi-circle of rubberneckers formed behind the Hellers.

Larry exhaled.

"It's funny," Margaret said. "Those Heller Boys are always causing trouble, but the only one the cops are really after is Slappy."

"Why's that funny?"

"He's the nicest one."

Larry thought so too, and he almost said that Bill and Mike weren't so bad either, but then he might have to explain, and he didn't want to open up that can of worms.

"It's not just that he's a good tipper," she said, "and he's so grateful when you make him a fancy cocktail. You can just feel it, deep down, he's a good guy. It's not his fault."

Larry nodded. He wanted to ask her what she felt about him, deep down, but he wasn't sure of her answer. Just a little farther, when they got far enough away from the square, he'd spill his guts. Then he'd know for sure how she felt about him, deep down.

"Who knows?" She said. "Maybe Casey will violate parole or something and be back in prison by the time Cheese Days is over."

"I can't wait for it to be over." All the hustling behind the bar was draining him, leaving him sore all over, aggravating his injuries.

"You gotta like the dough, though."

"Yeah, that part is good."

"You gonna use it to get your own place?"

He gave her a sidelong glance. She kept her eyes aimed forward, her hands in her pockets. He supposed he would use his small stake to move on, either to an apartment of his own, or he'd burn through it fleeing to another state. "Maybe."

"How is Mrs. Reeves? Is she gonna be ready for the big cheese contests tomorrow?"

He snorted. This weekend was the big finale of the festival, a fact that his landlady never seemed to shut up about. "She's better. Working around the clock to get ready. She's a tough old bird."

"People forget there's life after Cheese Days."

He felt a glimmer of hope. She must've meant for the two of them. He steeled himself, told himself that after this approaching car passed them, he'd spill his guts

He lifted his forearm in front of his eyes to ward off the headlights' dazzling beams, which reached a blinding apex, then diminished. The cruiser rolled parallel to them, and Officer Jim, patrolling alone, staring at them, tapped his index finger on the face of his wristwatch.

Larry blanched, not knowing how he was gonna explain to her.

"*Tchah.*" Margaret crossed her arms under her boobs. "Keeping an eye on me in case your gang of hoodlums tries to jump me."

85

"I'll protect you. You don't need to rely on your ex-boyfriends."

"I can take care of myself. I should've know better than to date a customer."

Larry frowned. His image of their prom court had felt so solid. "I've never seen him in the pub."

"Not anymore. You know how it goes, start off as friends, mess around a little, then break up over something stupid. Wouldn't be so bad, but somebody's feelings always get hurt, and that ruins the friendship, then they stop coming around. Probably better that way, though. Don't have to deal with all those uncomfortable moments, the dirty looks, all that crap."

"Yeah." He suspected that she wasn't only talking about customers. Everything she said could apply to coworkers too.

They reached the head of her walkway before he was ready. He was midway through a deep inhale when she touched his hand while saying, "Good night."

He watched her disappear within. No invitation to come inside, not even a kiss, add that to what she just said …

Her neat little house shimmered. He wiped his eyes, took a hitching breath, and started homeward. He peered upward at the treetops. He began to jog, gritting his teeth against the pain.

Chapter Eighteen

Larry guided the Olds past Margaret's little white house. The gray-black storm clouds fabricated a premature dusk, but all her windows showed darkness. She wasn't home. He'd worked the day shift to max out his cash reserves, in case Bill couldn't come up with the balance of what he owed before Larry's next court date passed and the judge issued a contempt warrant. He'd resisted the urge to linger after the shift in order to see her one last time. Officer Jim's deadline loomed.

He forced his eyes back towards the street. This little detour was stupid. It wasn't like he was gonna knock on her door, confess, and sweep her off her feet. He needed to get the hell out of town. Hell, he needed to figure out where he was gonna go.

From behind, a siren's half-whoop made him jump. The image of a squad car grew in his rearview mirror. He pounded the steering wheel. He should've known better. For a blink, he considered punching it, instigating a high-speed chase, going out in fiery wreck, then he took his foot off the gas and angled the Olds toward the curb. Maybe the prick wouldn't search his trunk and find the remainder of his pot hidden under the wheel well.

He shut off the Olds' engine. He kept his eyes aimed at the rearview. Probably Officer Jim wanted to stick it to him one last time, tell him that's what happens when you sniff around our women, some hardass bullshit. Or maybe the prick wanted to remind him to keep his mouth shut about giant squirrels, warn him that buddies in police departments all across the land would love to receive information on suspected drug dealers. Or maybe the whole damned thing was a setup, a way to catch him in possession of drugs and send him to prison.

The patrol car's door swung open. Larry gripped the steering wheel with both hands and squeezed as hard as he could. He guessed he'd know soon enough. The cop levered himself out of the car. Brown hair, mustache, not Officer Jim. Larry frowned. The cop, empty-handed, made a cautious approach on the Olds' driver side.

When the cop reached his window, Larry looked up into his grim face. The cop said, "You made your point. Call off the dogs."

Larry's scalp tingled. He suppressed the compulsion to scratch.

"We got the message," the cop said. "We're backing off."

"I'm sorry Officer, but I don't have the foggiest idea of what you're talking about."

"This isn't a setup. Just tell whoever needs to know. Tell them to back off."

The cop marched back to his car. As the cruiser pulled away, Larry marveled that Mike and Bill actually pulled it off. He'd just assumed Bill had been full of shit, that they just wanted him to stick around so they could squeeze another shipment or two out of him before he went to jail. He mumbled, "Yeah, but what exactly did they do?"

Chapter Nineteen

Larry piloted the Olds through the gauntlet of parked cars, which lined both sides of the gravel road, starting at least a half a mile before the Hellers' lane. He'd given up the search for a good spot, but he kept the Olds' speed a hair above idling, so as to negotiate the narrows created by crooked park-jobs, and by road-hogging vans and pickups.

From the west, shouts and laughter and heavy metal rang out over the crunch of gravel and the rumble of the Olds' engine. He rolled perpendicular to the lane. Cars jammed both sides of the rutted dirt all the way to the bend, at least, with many canting on the banks of the grassy ditches. He figured during the later stages of the party, a pack of mischievous drunks would form and go car tipping, flipping one or two beaters into the corn.

He continued north. About a half mile down the road the lineup of vehicles began to thin. He parked and sat behind the wheel, listening to the cooling engine tick. *Two birds with one stone.* He wasn't worried about making things clear to Meryl. The way Margaret had smiled, earlier on this final night of Cheese Days, when she came in for her shift and declared, 'We need to talk, *tomorrow*,' … that demand, in light of her steadily warming attitude since the night she abandoned him on the sidewalk, he could only interpret to mean good things.

His grinning lips leveled. After his shift, after Margaret's demand, Bub had called him aside and informed him that one of the mainstay bartenders was retiring after the festival, and so some night shifts were opening up. Night shifts meant good tips, a livable income. But then Bub had given him the hairy eyeball, and said, 'They're yours, but you gotta knock off the dealing.' Bub had stalked away before Larry could even begin to bluster a protest. He intended to be honest with Meryl. On the way out, he'd dissected all the excuses he could think of, but he kept coming back to the same approach, that he'd be honest with Mike too. The Hellers would have to find another connection.

He got out of the Olds and took a step towards the ditch, as if to cut through the field, then he remembered this was giant squirrel country. He tromped up the gravel and told himself that all these people surely frightened off any wild animals in the region, including giant squirrels. A shrill voice inside his head kept bringing up that the squirrels had braved a festival-clogged town to come after him. He sped up to a jogging pace. His still-healing left knee felt a little weak, but he didn't slow to a walk until the reached the Hellers' lane.

The breeze brought the savor of roast pork to his nose. He sensed a fragile calm as he walked between the dark vacant cars along this deserted leg before the bend. An urge to pause, to take a moment, welled up in him. He told himself to stop being chickenshit, and he soldiered on.

He rounded the bend and gaped. Like the first Heller shindig that he had attended, the windows of the small farmhouse were dark upstairs and glowing red downstairs. But this time a bonfire illuminated the near side of the house. A half-shredded hog, a spit skewering the carcass from ass to skull and raising the remains four feet off the ground, loomed in front of the fire. Around the corner on the north side of the house a moshpit churned to Anthrax, the pit bigger than some Larry had seen at metal shows. Gentler headbangers circled the pit whiplashing their shaggy heads while some spun out of the throng to catch their breath, and others dived back into the tribal chaos.

Revelers collected around the parked cars, leaning, sitting on hoods, drinking, hooting, snarfing platefuls of barbecue, paying him no mind as he passed. Closer to the house, folks sat on hay bales around the stuck hog, playing cards and chomping on pork sandwiches. Potluck dishes, buns, paper plates, bags of chips, and condiments loaded two picnic tables beside the hog. Folks gnawed fried corn on the cob and shoveled in spoonfuls of grilled potatoes and homemade pork and beans. Near the carcass, the smack of burnt animal fat thickened.

Larry estimated there might be three hundred attendees. Everyone seemed to hold a cup of beer, or a bottle of beer, or a wine cooler, or a two-liter pop bottle sloshing with liquids that Larry knew were juiced with generous doses of booze. Even the small packs of little kids, dark-eyed and stringy-looking, their parents bringing them along for the ride, ran wild while clutching soda cans in their hands.

He circumnavigated the moshpit and reached the propped-open front door of the house. He turned sideways and shouldered his way through the jammed porch and into the kitchen. A red haze skimmed the top of his head. Anthrax blared from the living room. Bottlenecked, he noted all the beards and mustaches. At least this time around the majority of partygoers seemed of legal drinking age.

He went up on his toes and looked toward the living room. In the doorway between rooms, two dudes about Larry's height parted. Barney, mirrored shades hiding his eyes, lorded over the stereo. The crowd shifted, and Larry lost sight of the little asshole.

Larry rotated and worked himself out of the house. He breathed in a lungful of fresh air. A current of partygoers budged him to the back corner of the house before he realized he was in the keg line.

A worklight, outfitted with a red bulb, clamped to the awning overhead, radiated down on two, waist-high, corrugated-aluminum washtubs. Each tub held three tapped kegs of various brews, and gallons of slushy ice. A pyramid of empty kegs leaned against the backside of the house. A couple of untapped kegs, one on top of the other, sat on a cast-iron dolly behind the tubs. The line disgorged the freshly beered partygoers into the grassy area between the keg station and the barns.

Jay-Jay, manning the keg station, was slammed. Larry noted the mistakes the poor little dude made, each tiny mistake decreasing efficiency, as he struggled to keep up with the impatient customers. Larry knew he could jump in and kill the line in five minutes flat. Instead, he enjoyed watching somebody else work his ass off for a change, although he couldn't help feeling a little sorry for Jay-Jay by the time he reached the front of the line. Now that he had seen Jay-Jay in the light of day, he couldn't unsee those weird eyes, with the round right socket and almond-shaped left. Jay-Jay had sweated through his black Metallica tee shirt. Larry nodded and ordered a Miller. Jay-Jay, sneering, charged Larry three bucks for the cup.

Larry sipped his beer and joined a group of recently-served partiers who were gathered next to the tubs and roaring with laughter. He craned his neck to catch a glimpse of what they were laughing at. Slappy, crouching, jumped like a frog, back and forth from behind the tubs and into view, while holding his hands near his chest and wriggling his fingers, and scrunching his eyes and baring his teeth. He made guttural noises that sounded like, "Nyng, nyng-nyng," over and over. One of the looky-loos said, "He's doing the Evil Gremlin."

Slappy spotted Larry and bounded out of his crouch. The small crowd parted for him as he pinwheeled his arm for balance. Larry managed to catch and steady Slappy without spilling too much beer.

Larry muddled through Slappy's sudsy, prolonged greeting, then said, "You got quite a crowd."

"Hell, yeah! Our end of Cheese Days parties are famous!"

Larry looked over the grounds. "You aren't afraid of the cops?"

"*Shee-yit!*" Slappy leaned in close and dropped his voice to a whisper. "That cop got what he had comin' to him."

Larry nodded. He hadn't asked Bill. He figured he'd better leave well enough alone. Hadn't taken long for word to spread that somebody kicked the shit out of good old Officer Jim. The way Larry figured it, the rest of Murray's police force jumped to the conclusion that he was mobbed up. If that kept them off his back, he was fine with it. He said, "So, where is everyone? Where's Bill?"

"I dunno," Slappy swiveled his head. "He's around here somewhere."

"Is Meryl around?

Slappy shot Larry a lopsided smirk. "Oh yeah. I bet she can't wait to see you."

"Yeah, with work and all, I just never got the time to come by …"

"Gotta go!"

Slappy dashed behind the tubs. Jay-Jay shouted something at him, and Slappy hurried around the corner.

Larry shrugged. He stepped back as the keg line continued to eject customers. The barn area seemed deserted except for those who were looking for a little privacy in order to take a whiz. The other freshly-served partygoers were milling toward the north side of the house, some, he didn't doubt, to get right back in the beer line. He decided to go against the grain and he looped around the south side. Here, the corn ranged within five feet of the house, leaving a swath of high grass in between. The shut windows muffled the speed-metal

92

rhythms. A tree partially obstructed the far corner of the house, creating the illusion of a peaceful grove.

Larry halted in the middle of the deserted swath and looked up at the second floor. He located the window of the room where Meryl had taken him that first time. He wondered how long that giant squirrel had sat on the sill and peeped at them.

He glanced at the reddened first-floor windows. People crammed the living room wall-to-wall. He was not about to fight his way through the interior of the house while searching for Bill and Meryl. He edged around the tree and found himself behind the hog carcass.

The windows were shut on this side of the house too, sparing the older partiers from the brunt of the blistering metal spewing out on the north side. Larry's stomach rumbled, but after he wandered around the food, and saw the ravaged state of the condiments and side dishes, a state of thorough cross-contamination, he decided to stick with his beer. For a moment he thought of going for some roast pork, but seeing the hog corpse sagging on the spit, with great hunks of flesh torn out of the prime locations, charred rib bones showing through, a beer can shoved into its flame-broiled snout, and its eye sockets hollow but gooey, he decided he would never eat pork again.

He wandered among the card players. Most sat on the ground around hay bales that were used as card tables. Some played euchre, some played poker, and one group played a drinking game they called 'Take Five' here Illinois, but back home, Larry and his buddies called it 'Up the River, Down the River.' Larry guessed that whatever anybody called it, it was the most brutal drinking game he'd ever played. Still, neither Meryl nor Bill was among the gamers, or the people hanging around the gamers.

He drifted to the north and east, away from the party, toward the lane. He finished his beer, dropped the cup in the grass, not feeling the slightest twinge of remorse after seeing all the litter on the three occupied sides of the house, and he started down the lane.

He maintained a casual gait as he passed people. He nodded to those he recognized. He crossed paths with two separate groups of latecomers. When he reached the bend, he accelerated. He was at the gatepost when he heard, "Where ya going so fast?"

He wiped the wistful smile off his face and turned around. Meryl was strutting towards him, her hips taking their own sweet time in switching from side to side. She was wearing pumps that gave her an extra inch, cut-offs so skimpy that the bottom of the pockets stuck out, and a dark tube-top, which gave a tight jiggle with every step. It just wasn't fair.

"Well?" she asked, as she zeroed in on him.

He was three steps toward her before he realized he was walking. "I didn't see you around, so I was gonna take off."

"Been so long since I've seen you, I thought you forgot all about me."

He tried to look away, but the best he could do was to shift his eyes from her hips to her breasts, then to her face. "Are you mad at me?"

"Yeah, I am."

They stopped within arm's reach. "Why?"

"You know why." She stared up at him, showing whites around the bottom of her eyes.

He braced himself, then said, "Listen, we gotta talk."

She took a half-step inward. She smelled like peaches. "Uh-oh, I don't like the sound of that."

He studied her face. Her small mouth, her shiny eyes, indicated no shock, no surprise. She knew. "I want to clear the air."

Her eyes misted up. "Yep."

He laid his palms on her shoulders. "I think you're great. Really great. But ..."

"But there's someone else."

He sucked in a harsh breath, then nodded.

A tear rolled down her cheek, yet her voice was even and resigned, when she said, "It was bound to happen."

"I'm sorry. I didn't mean for it to happen, and I would've told you sooner, but ..."

"I know." She stepped forward and nestled the side of her head against his chest. She wrapped her arms around him. "You're a good guy, Larry. Not a great guy, but a good guy for sure."

He returned her hug, then released her.

She stepped back, still holding his right hand in her left. She bit her lower lip and raised an eyebrow. "One more time, for the road?"

"W-what?"

With her right hand she reached forward and rubbed him between the legs. He hardened. She rasped, "You can't tell me you don't wanna."

He hissed in a shivery breath as, over his jeans, she rotated his stiffening cock to its upright position, then caressed the underside with deep upstrokes.

He gasped. It was wrong, but he didn't make a move to stop her. He closed his eyes. Seconds later, he assured himself that starting tomorrow, everything would change. He would change. He opened his eyes. "Oh, God. I guess one last time won't hurt."

She led him between two parked cars and through several rows of corn. After a brief skirmish with his inhibition against doing it outside, only yards away from hundreds of people, he surrendered to reckless abandon. If he was gonna cheat, and he knew damned well he was lying to himself when he cited technicalities, technicalities like when he avowed that there was no verbal agreement in place, if he was really gonna go through with it, then by God he was gonna *do it*.

He fucked her brains out. The first time standing, her legs coiled around his hips, her heels digging into his butt cheeks, their ferocious thrusts creating audible slaps. The second time he spun her around and she bent over and grabbed her ankles.

He pulled his pants up his shaky legs. He'd only had the one beer so he couldn't cry 'drunk.' Fresh sweat beaded on his hot forehead. They shouldn't have done this. *He* shouldn't have done this. While buckling his belt, while repeating his silent vow to be a better man starting tomorrow, a rustling in the corn froze him. He grabbed her arm and whispered, "Did you hear that?"

She listened, then laughed. "The wind. Or somebody watching the show."

"Or a giant squirrel."

She scoffed. "Put your shirt on. It's time to go."

He didn't argue. Fully-clothed, they stole out of the corn where they'd entered. Three shapes emerged from behind a pickup and stood in their path. Larry recognized Jackie, shirtless, and Barney, still wearing those mirrored shades. The third stood a good foot taller than Barney, and from Larry's perspective, at the bottom of the ditch, the big dude seemed like a giant. His snarled hair plastered against his skull. His sleeveless jean-jacket hung unbuttoned over his rippling, shirtless torso. The cuffs of his skintight jeans tucked into his black combat boots. A black leather band wrapped around each wrist. His fists seemed huge. *Casey.*

The smaller Hellers slouched against the pickup and folded their arms across their chests. Casey stood at the edge of the ditch, glaring down on Larry and Meryl, his chest puffed out, tightening and loosening his fists, pumping up his rounded biceps. He said, "Well, well, well. This must be the great and wonderful Larry." He looked Larry up and down. Larry had never felt so puny. "You wanna tell me what you're doing in the corn with little sister?"

"I'm not *your* sister," Meryl said.

"Close enough," Casey said. His head waggled as he regarded Larry. "So we pull your drawers down, your pecker gonna be all stanked up?"

Meryl gasped, "Casey!"

Casey let himself drop half a yard down the ditch bank.

Meryl stepped in front of Larry. "Let him be!"

Casey murmured, "Well, well."

"See?" Barney said. "I told'ja."

"Listen man," Larry said. "I'm not looking for any trouble."

Casey hawked and spat. He hopped the rest of the way down the ditch, bopping to a stop in front of Meryl. His eyes never left Larry. Casey's pungent BO made Larry wince. Casey seized Meryl by the shoulders. She yelped as he lifted her up and set her to the side.

On even ground, Larry was nearly eye-to-eye with Casey, but he estimated he was spotting at least thirty pounds, all thirty rock-hard muscle.

"We broke up!" Meryl said. "We're not gonna do it anymore!"

Casey glanced at her. "Good to see you came to your senses." He jabbed his index finger at Larry. "But you, mothafucka, you done crossed the line."

Meryl darted up the ditch and weaved between two parked cars.

Larry held his palms out. "I don't wanna fight you man."

Casey took a forward step, and Larry backed up. He felt corn leaves brushing his ass. He glanced past Casey. Barney and Jackie started down the ditch. "C'mon, three against one?"

96

"They're just here to make sure you don't run away," Casey said.

Barney and Jackie snickered. Casey torpedoed Larry. They crashed into the corn, mashing down a strip of stalks. Casey planted Larry on his back. Casey squirmed on top of Larry, who strained, but Casey was too heavy. Casey pinned Larry's left shoulder under his knee, then worked his other knee over Larry's right shoulder. Casey reared up and cocked his right fist next to his ear.

Casey panted while laughing. He puffed, "You're fucked." Casey ratcheted his fist back then unleashed it. Larry squeezed his eyes shut. The punch clipped the side of his jaw as Casey's weight lurched off of his chest. He scrambled to his feet.

Mike disentangled himself from Casey and sprang to his feet. "What the fuck is wrong with you?"

Casey popped up and stamped on crushed cornstalks while crowding Mike nose-to-nose. The rest of the Hellers arrived at the crest of a wave of partygoers, who streamed between parked cars and formed a semicircle of jostling, gleeful spectators, sealing off every avenue of escape but the cornfield.

Casey shoved Mike, who stepped right back into Casey's face. Casey said, "This been comin' ever since I got out. Come get your whippin', flatdick."

"I'm not a little kid anymore," Mike said. "Might be harder than it used to be."

Over the crowd's growing chant of "Fight! Fight!", Casey shouted, while waving towards Larry, "Why you takin' that mothafucka's part?"

"You're a moron," Mike said.

Casey pointed at Larry and said, "Don't you go nowhere. Soon as I'm done with this little cocksucker, you're next."

Meryl screamed, "Stop it!"

Larry tracked her voice. Jackie and Barney held her back at the edge of the crowd. He surveyed the pumping fists, the chanters, their blood-lusting faces, and he saw only one way out. He stepped beside Mike and said, "This coward caught me off guard. I get first crack."

Casey bared his crooked yellow teeth. He called out loud enough for everyone to hear, "I'll take both you cunts on, one after the other."

A symphonized "Wuuuuuu" rose from the crowd, roller-coastering through pitches before crashing into discordant laughter.

Larry thumped his fist against his chest. "Me first."

The mob's chanting synched up into another chorus of "Fight! Fight!"

"You sure about this?" Mike asked.

Casey shouted, "C'mon, let's get the fucking show on the road."

Larry nodded to Mike, who shook his head and backed away. Larry squared up with Casey, who kept his eyes on Mike while saying, "Don't go too far, little brother."

Larry reminded himself that he had eighty-sixed plenty of guys bigger than Casey. He reminded himself to be fast. He turned sideways to Casey. He brought his fists up and bent his knees into that old fighting stance. Casey stood with his feet shoulder-width apart, opening and clenching his fists, popping his biceps, his lips curled into a snarling smile.

Larry slitted his eyes. Casey's nonchalant stance meant he didn't respect him. *Good.*

Casey began to circle while closing in. Larry mirrored him until they had exchanged original positions. Larry found the frenzied crowd difficult to block out. He was afraid his focus was slipping. Again, he told himself to be fast, and to throw the first punch.

With his left, Larry back-fisted Casey's nose. Casey blinked and took a backward step. With his right, Larry stepped into a straight punch aimed at Casey's nose. Before the punch landed, the motion felt as comfortable and practiced as it did back in karate class, when Sensei made him and his fellow students throw thousands of punches into the air, while picking every little nit in their forms. He twisted his hips, kept his shoulders relaxed, and corkscrewed his fist from supine to prone right before impact, adding extra torque to the blow. Sensei would have been proud.

The violence of the collision shocked Larry, and he let up just a little on the follow-through. Still, he felt cartilage smashing under his knuckles.

Casey staggered back and fluttered his arms for balance, but he still fell flat on his ass. Blood gushed from his mangled nose. The crowd thundered while Casey sat there cross-eyed. He brought his hands together, covering the lower half of his face, but blood oozed down his chin and drizzled onto his chest.

Barney rushed over to help him up, but Casey shoved him away with one hand. He tottered up to his feet, then wiped his muzzle and flicked blood onto the grass.

The crowd cheered.

Larry kept his fists up and remained angled to Casey, leading with his left shoulder. Casey hawked and spat a wad of blood into the grass, then, with a howl, he charged. Possible counters flashed through Larry's mind, then he side-stepped and let Casey pass untouched. He told himself not to think so much.

Casey wheeled. Larry closed in, and threw a punch at Casey's face, but Casey bobbed out of the way and landed an uppercut to Larry's ribcage. Larry grunted, dropped his elbows, a tardy reflex, then raised his fists and forearms as Casey unleashed a furious flurry. Casey hammered Larry's arms into his own face, often and forceful enough to stagger Larry. The blows stopped, and a split-second later the bottom dropped out of Larry's world. Casey had punched Larry in the nuts.

As a flinching "Ooooooh!" rose from the males in the crowd, Larry dropped to his knees, his hands covering his crotch too late. Somebody nearby shouted, "What the fuck was that?" Larry looked up. Casey was winding up for a massive haymaker. Larry got his arms up in time to block the onset of the blow, but the follow-through knocked him onto his back.

Mike yelled, "Enough! That's enough!"

Casey crowed, "I'm not even close to through with him."

Larry rolled to his side, cradled his balls, brought his knees up, and tucked his head. He gaped fishlike, and tried to find the bottom of his stomach. He was helpless and he knew it. He hoped that if he didn't fight back, somebody would stop the massacre before it got too bad.

The mob whooped. He opened his eyes and turned his head. Mike and Casey were tangled in the corn. A foot came down on his ankle. He rolled up onto his knees, his forehead touching the grass, his hands clamped over the back of his head as the mob trampled around him. When the worst of it passed, after taking a few heels to the back and ass, he struggled to rise to his feet. He stood, his palms on his knees to support his upper body, and he panted.

He was near the rear of the mob now, the bulk having reformed near the corn-line. He couldn't see the combatants, but judging by the hoots and hollers, the brawl was in full swing.

Soon he was standing alone. He vomited. He concentrated on recapturing his breath, barely registering the din. Then flashing red lights flickered across his field of vision. He thought he was passing out until the mob churned around him. Everybody seemed to be yelling "Cops!" as they jostled past him.

Someone banged into his shoulder from behind and shoved him out of the way. He stumbled and righted himself as Casey swaggered up the ditch with Barney and Jackie in tow. Casey looked back, his face and hair streaked with blood and dirt. "I ain't forgot about you."

Barney looked back at Larry and said, "Yeah," as the trio marched towards the house.

The cops blockaded the lane, leaving the red lights flashing while they reconnoitered the party. Somebody turned off the music. Larry, among others, sat on a bale of hay, and kept his head down. He didn't see any Hellers as the cops hassled random adults, the minors having already fled into the corn. The cops pretended not to notice the giggles and the whispers of the drunken idiots, as well as their stalk-rending falls.

Finally, Mike, wearing a clean set of clothes, his face washed and his hair combed, emerged from the house and conferred with the officers. Larry was close enough to hear Mike agree to pulling the plug, letting a few people out at a time, so there wouldn't be a hundred drunk drivers on the road all at once.

The cops left without busting anyone or writing a single ticket. The minors returned from the corn. Mike ordered the music back on, and didn't order anyone to leave. The party warmed, then percolated to near its former zeal. The card games resumed, the moshpit reformed under the satanic riffage of Mercyful Fate, and dudes lined up for beer.

All the while Larry looked to make a break for it, but his efforts were thwarted by guys cornering him and slapping him on the back, asserting that Larry would've kicked Casey's ass if not for that low blow. They imitated Larry's combination, the one-two move that put Casey on his butt, and asked Larry for pointers. Fans handed

Larry beers and half-pints of both liqueurs and harder stuff, and several joints were passed his way.

He kept inching towards the lane, growing a little more drunk, a little more stoned, with each foot gained. Reeling by the time he'd made it partway down the first leg of the rutted lane, he glanced over the shoulders of the three-deep crowd barring his way and saw her coming around the bend.

Somewhere in his fogged higher functions he knew it was stupid to try to hide. He was the talk of the party, and somebody would tell Margaret all about it before she could down her first beer. But his lower functions seized control.

His fans, perhaps sensing his constant probing for an avenue of escape, had thickened on the down-lane side. He mumbled that he had to take a piss, spun around, and shoved through the thin ranks of well-wishers who had been standing behind him. He hurried to the barns, ignoring the people calling out to him along the way.

From the corner of the first barn he spied on Margaret and her friends as they went through the process of getting beers. He groped for an excuse, something he could tell her that would make it all right. He was too fucked up for the job. *Tomorrow.* Tomorrow was his only hope. He could only make things worse tonight.

He squinted into the darkness behind himself. He figured that beyond the barns, the corn started up. He could cut unseen across the fields and drive home, and deal with this mess after a good night's sleep.

Moonbeams spotlighted a small patch ahead, but the awnings and eaves of the odd collection of barns blotted out the rest of the sky and cast deep shadows before him. He slunk forward, trailing the fingers of his left hand along the splintery wood of barn's wall, his only guide in the darkness. When he reached the end of the wall he stepped out into space, his hands out in front of him like a blind man. After several nervy steps, he touched wood. He turned south and felt his way along the wall. He reached the corner and stopped, holding his breath.

Somewhere nearby liquid pattered against dirt. He edged around the corner and along the barn, certain that the pisser would return this way when finished. His fingers found an open doorway in time to save him from bumping his head into a slightly ajar door. He nudged the door till the opening was wide enough for him to squeeze through. He slid inside.

The barn reeked of dusty animal spoor. He blinked, but his eyes could not adjust to the blackness. From above, wood creaked.

Jackie whispered, "Just somebody takin' a piss. They're gone now."

Casey, also whispering, said, "Good."

Larry located their voices above his head and against the wall. He figured they chose to hide from the cops on a hay mow.

Barney whispered, "He's gone too far this time."

"As soon as you were gone," Jackie said, "he started changin' things."

"Started pimpin' her out," Barney said.

"That dirty mothafucka," Casey said. "He's gonna fuck everything up."

"He shouldn't even be in charge," Barney said.

"That's why the mothafucka talked me into turning myself in," Casey said. "Fuck. I can't believe how fucking stupid I was. He told me we can't make waves, and the whole time I was inside, Slappy's running free, and those guys are jumpin' cops. Fuck!"

"Greedy motherfucka," Jackie said.

"Yeah," Casey said. "I bet he was hopin' I'd fuck up, lose my parole. Fuck. You know what would'a happened then?"

"It would'a all been over," Barney said.

"Damn right! I'm the oldest, next to Slappy. I got less time. He should wait his fucking turn, like it's always been."

Wood creaked again. Larry imagined one of them rising from his haunches.

"What're we gonna do?" Barney said. "He won't stop on his own."

Casey sniffed. "Let's cut off his supply."

"Yeah?" Barney asked.

"Yeah. That particular mothafucka has it comin'. This way, we hit Mikey-boy right where it hurts."

"Awesome," Jackie said.

"Yeah," Barney said. "Yeah, that's good."

"It's settled then," Casey said. "We act cool. I mean, I was drunk, right? Just got a little out'a hand, that's all. When he gets comfortable again, then motherfuckin' bam!"

"Fuck yeah," Barney said. "Fuck, yeah!"

"Cool," Casey said. "Now you guys get your asses back to the party, and act like everything's hunky-dory. I'm gonna go get me some muff."

The other two chuckled. Footsteps clomped across the boards above. Larry pressed himself against the wall and slid away from the door. The thumping stopped almost directly overhead, then Larry marked their descent by the wooden groans and squeaks of the rickety ladder, a ladder close enough that Larry could reach out and touch it. Underneath this racket, a sizzle hissed from the mow. His hackles rose, and he flinched when the sizzling ended in a pulpy *pock*.

He shook off his squeamishness at the nerve-scraping sound. He was more worried about the Hellers who climbed down the ladder with ease and confidence, as if they could see in the dark. He flattened himself against the wall. He felt the air displacement as they jumped to the plank floor and passed him on their way out. The door swung back and forth on its hinges, which grated through a series of diminishing, rusty whines.

He held his breath while waiting for Casey to come down, but all was quiet overhead. He began counting to a hundred. At thirty-eight, he went for the door. He stopped and listened. The barns dampened the party hullabaloo. Sounded like the coast was clear.

He felt his way along the barn, moving west. When he reached the end of the barn he could see moonlight to the south. There was a narrow alley between his barn and the next, the alley leading to the cornfield. He took the alley straight into the corn. The rows ran east-west. He pushed south through a dozen rows, just to be safe, then turned east toward the gravel road. He hurried down the row. The tassels swished high enough so that he didn't need to duck. Whispers, a little to his left in the corn between him and the house, stopped him dead in his tracks.

He recognized their voices, but he couldn't make out what they were saying. Mike, Bill, and Slappy. Larry deduced from their clipped utterances that they were arguing. He cursed himself for not working his way to the north side of the barns, where he could've taken a straight shot through the corn to his car.

He squatted, then he sagged all the way down in the soil. The thrash metal grinding out of the house butchered their exact words, then Slappy raised his voice, saying, "I gotta!" The initial crashing through stalks softened, the more stealthy whisks marking the position of a loner as he slunk deeper into the corn.

Larry's heartbeat thrummed in his ears. He watched Slappy pass through his row maybe ten yards in front of him. Slappy didn't look his way, but stole on, pushing stalks aside without uprooting or snapping them.

Larry glanced up and down his empty row. Mike and Bill weren't following Slappy. In a matter of minutes he could be driving away from this nightmare. His adrenaline waned, and a massive headrush dizzied him. God he was wasted. Maybe just a little more exercise would sober him up. Anyways, Slappy might know what the hell Casey was planning. He stood and charted an intercepting course, slipping between cornstalks.

Slappy had stopped another dozen rows away. Larry eased a few low corn leaves out of his line of sight. Slappy had hung his ballcap on a stalk, the tassel poking through the hole in back. Larry frowned. Slappy shucked off his shirt, revealing a fishbelly-white back. He kicked off his sneakers, then bent over, balanced on one foot, and pulled up his ankle. He removed his sock, then repeated the maneuver for the other foot.

Slappy unzipped his jeans. Larry shook his head, thinking that maybe Slappy had a secret rendezvous arranged with some woman. He couldn't think of any other reason why anybody would be getting naked in the cornfield.

Slappy stepped out of his jeans. His tighty-whities pouched a little in the ass. Larry grimaced. Slappy should've known better, he should've worn clean underwear, if he was meeting up with a woman out here. Larry didn't want to look, but he couldn't look away as Slappy shimmied out of his underwear, which he hung on the stalk, a node below his hat.

Slappy's bare butt gleamed in the moonlight. Larry began to turn away. He certainly didn't want to watch Slappy bang some chick, which was the best-case scenario for whatever the crazy bastard was up to.

Tremors seized Slappy. He moaned. His muscles exploded into stunning definition. He hunched over, and shook and spasmed down onto all fours. A short sizzle preceded a pulpy *pock*. The monster squirrel bolted deeper into the corn and out of sight.

Chapter Twenty

Larry opened his eyes. He was face-to-face with the dusty underside of the Olds' dashboard. The tapping on the driver's side window, that's what woke him up. He shifted his head and the sunlight reflecting off the side mirror blinded him. He groaned and raised his hand to shield his face. His calves wedged between the driver's seat and the steering wheel, his back flat on the passenger side's floorboards, he gripped the armrest and hauled himself up. He stared at the driver's window until the blur outside the window sharpened into Margaret's royally pissed-off face.

He mumbled "What ...?"

Margaret, her voice muffled by the closed window, but her wrath loud and clear, said, "Unlock the door!"

He struggled up into a sitting position. He blinked and rubbed his throbbing forehead.

She shouted, "Open the door!"

He unlocked the door and swung it open.

Tears welled up in her eyes. "You're an asshole!"

He rubbed his forehead. "What?" Then it hit him.

"I just wanted you to know that I never want to see you again!" She whirled and began stomping away.

"Wait." He staggered up from the driver's seat. His stomach sloshed. He steadied himself on the door. "Wait, Margaret."

She lashed around. "What? What can you say?"

He dropped his gaze. Dirt and pulpy green striped his shirt and jeans, his scabbed right kneecap showed through a ragged hole. He looked up at her. "Please, just let me explain. Please. Hear me out. Then if you don't wanna have anything to do with me, I'll understand."

She planted her fists on her hips and glared at him. Her cheekbones flexed as she ground her teeth behind sealed lips. Finally, she said, "Okay."

His shoulders dropped. "Can we go somewhere, somewhere private?"

"You can drive me home. I'll give you that far. First, I have to tell my ride that I'm leaving. I can't *wait* to hear you try and talk yourself out of this one."

Before he could thank her, she'd wheeled her back to him. She strode down the gravel road.

Larry closed his eyes. Tomorrow had come far too soon. He was not ready for this. He squinted his eyes open. Cars still dotted both sides of the road, but on this morning after, two or three, and sometimes four, car-lengths separated them. He looked at his watch and groaned again. Less than five hours to go before he had to be at work.

He doddered away from the sun and gazed over the green expanse of corn. The corn. Slappy, naked. He shook his feverish head. He'd been so wasted last night that he'd thought he saw … he'd seen a giant squirrel. He'd seen Slappy and a giant squirrel out in the corn, and somehow his inebriated mind … it was the opposite of seeing double.

He sighed, and felt a little better. He'd been drunk, maybe a little punch drunk, it'd been dark, Slappy and the giant squirrel had been near each other, and the last thing he remembered … he must've passed out. Somebody found him in the corn, and took him back to his car. Simple.

He had a hazy memory of rolling up the windows and locking the doors … he jumped back to naked Slappy. He snorted. He smiled, recalling how white Slappy's skin had been, how his ass had glowed in the moonlight. He stopped smiling. You don't get naked while you're waiting for a woman in the middle of a cornfield. You get naked because you're about to change into a giant squirrel, and you don't wanna get all tangled up in your human clothes. *That sound.* That sound had given him the willies. He shuddered.

He bent over and vomited into the ditch. His stomach contracted, heaved, contracted. He spat up the sludge in the back of his mouth, then spat again. He straightened up, sweating and shaking. "Oh God."

Rapid footsteps crunched gravel. He faced her approach. She hugged herself tightly. She stared at the road before her feet. He touched his sore stomach and felt dried dirt. He brushed at his shirt with the side of his hand. He ran his hand through his hair, and he dislodged a shred of cornleaf. He made a quick check of the rest of his hair, which seemed free of debris. His face was too stubbly to tell how dirty it might be.

He fished his keys out of his front pocket and held them out to her. Still tasting bile, he tried not to breathe in her face. "Can you drive? I don't think I can."

She snatched the keys and brushed past him. She dropped into the driver's seat and slammed the door shut. She started the Olds. She rolled down her window, then said, without looking at him, "You coming?"

He stumbled around the car and tried to open the locked passenger door. He tapped on the dusty window. She fired bitch-eyes at him. He suspected that she was considering whether or not to drive off without him.

She unlocked the door. He jumped in, and she pulled away before he could shut his door.

He cast about for a way to start. She lead-footed the gas pedal, and shards of gravel pinged off the Olds' undercarriage. She stared out the windshield. Instead of asking her to slow down, he reached out his right hand and gripped the dashboard.

Staring straight ahead, she said, "I'm waiting to hear why you think it's okay to have sex with a fourteen year-old girl."

He recoiled. But no denials rose to his lips. The truth of it was undeniable. The Hellers' hostility, the vague, taboo spice when they fucked … He gagged, then said, "She told me she was eighteen."

Margaret uttered a sharp laugh. "Yeah, right."

"I swear she did! I swear I didn't know! Listen, nobody said a word! It wasn't like we were dating each other, and the way she threw herself at me, right in front of them, and they didn't say 'boo.' We weren't seeing each other. We just … did it a few times …" As soon as that last bit was out of his mouth he knew he shouldn't have said it.

"That's why you didn't pressure me, you were getting some on the side." She glanced at him, then returned to staring at the road. "When did it start?"

"Before we … before."

"How many times after?"

"The reason I went out there last night was to end it."

"You know, if her parents gave half a damn, they could send you to jail."

"I didn't know." Yeah, but now that he thought about it, he remembered her making a joke about being fourteen. She only claimed to be joking after his shocked reaction.

"Bullshit. "How could you not know? Just one look would tell anybody …"

As she ticked off the obvious signs of Meryl's true age, his mind wandered to the Hellers. Their hostility not only made sense, but it made everything else make sense too. Slappy and Bill saw him and Margaret together at the pre-Cheese Days party. They told the others. They spied on him and Margaret from the treetops. Had to be them, because nobody else knew anything about their budding romance except maybe their co-workers. He mumbled, "She said she knew I was seeing somebody else." He rubbed his sand-papery chin. One, he'd been fucking their sister or cousin or whatever. Two, she happened to be fourteen. Three, they'd thought he was cheating on her. Three strikes. He nodded. So Barney, Jackie, and Jay-Jay, as monster squirrels, jumped him. It made perfect sense.

He twisted toward back her. She was saying, "I can't believe you never thought to ask how old–"

"LISTEN TO ME!" A burst of violent throbs assaulted his head.

She said, in a tense, quiet voice, "Okay. I'm listening."

"I saw something last night … they're gonna try to kill me."

She looked at him, then back at the road. "What the hell are you talking about?"

"Just listen. I should've told you this right from the start."

She eased off the gas pedal, but they were still rocketing down the road.

He cleared his throat. "It wasn't wild dogs that attacked me and Mrs. Reeves. It was monster squirrels."

She scowled. She stomped down on the gas pedal. She barked out a bitter laugh. "Oh my god!" She shook her head. "I thought you said you wanted to talk."

"Just listen! I told her the night before, about Reeves and how she drowns squirrels …"

"Drowns squirrels? What? What do squirrels have to do with *anything*?"

"The very next morning, they came after her. All of them. Wild animals wouldn't know any better … wild animals wouldn't take revenge … wild animals wouldn't know how to set up an ambush!"

She fumed. She slapped on the turn signal. The blinker pulsed audibly in the dead silence of car's interior. He grabbed the dashboard with his left hand, and re-gripped his right, and locked both elbows in preparation for the coming turn. She took her foot off the gas, but didn't bother to brake. She whipped the wheel. The Olds fishtailed onto the highway. He exhaled. She stepped on the gas.

He swallowed, then let his arms drop to his sides. "They were watching me. That's how she knew about me and you … and that was the last straw!" He turned back to her. "Don't you get it? They were watching us!"

She looked at him, her face composed, her eyes distant. "Should I drive you to the hospital?"

He stared her. She wasn't even listening. He imagined what he must look like. His dirty clothes, dirty hair, dirty face, and the hangover sleaze. He must look crazy. Still, he had to try. "I know how this looks. But they were mad enough at me as it was. And when they thought I was cheating on her … and there were three of them! Barney for sure, and Jackie, and Jay-Jay, probably."

"They thought you were cheating on *her*?"

"Yes! I heard them talking last night. It was the other three, Mike and Bill, and Slappy, probably, they got Officer Jim! Don't you see?" By the rage written all over her face he could see that she didn't. He couldn't see how he'd be able to explain that they change into giant squirrels, so that their victims don't have any idea of who attacked them, and so that their victims won't dare to even speak the truth about *what* attacked them. He couldn't see how he could tell her about that sizzle, like the sound a chicken breast makes when it's dropped into a pan of scorching oil. And that *pock*, like a bone popping out of a joint, the gristle ripping around it.

He looked at her. She stared at the road. The tires whined over the pavement. They'd be in Murray in a couple of minutes. "I think they're gonna try to kill me."

She didn't respond. As they entered the town he saw that it was useless. He wanted to tell her to slow down, at least take the corners slower, but the set of her jaw and the slant of her eyes convinced him to keep his mouth shut.

She parked the Olds in his customary spot in front of Mrs. Reeves house. He didn't look at her, and he could tell she wasn't looking at him. He said, "I don't know what to say."

"I thought you might finally tell me why you came to Murray."

He opened his mouth, about to reply, then he snapped it shut as a snippet of last night flickered in his mind's eye. Crawling between stalks, belly scraping soil, grass, gravel, throwing himself inside the car and locking the doors, weeping all the while …

"I guess I already know," She said. "Has something to do with drugs, right? What else could it be?" She put her hand on the door handle.

"No. It had nothing to do with drugs. But none of that matters right now. They might know that I know."

"How stupid do you think I am?"

He faced her. "Haven't you heard a word I said? They must know that I know! They're gonna try to kill me!"

"Maybe it's for the best if you run away again. I don't know how things would be at work. If you decide to stick around … just stay out of my way." She looked him in the eye and said, "Larry, don't ever speak to me again."

She got out of the car and walked away.

Chapter Twenty-one

Larry checked up and down the alley, then darted along the garage. He stopped at the corner and scanned the treetops. Still early evening, still broad daylight, they wouldn't dare come this far into town until nightfall, but nowadays he kept an eye on the treetops whenever he was outside.

They would kill him for sure if they saw him sneaking around here.

Drawn curtains blanked every window of the two-story yellow house. Dandelions speckled the backyard's longish grass. Between two red poles, an empty clothesline ran the length of the backyard. Beside the backdoor a black round-top grill stood on a cement patio.

He studied the house for any sign of life. He'd spent the last two days trying to come up with a better plan. Margaret still wouldn't look at him. She wasn't answering the phone. On the other hand, Bub came through with the promised nightshifts, and because Bub wasn't treating him any differently, even though it was obvious to everyone that she wasn't speaking to him, she must have said something to Bub on his behalf. So there was hope. Otherwise, he'd already be on the run, already be a fugitive from the law, not to mention from murderous monster squirrels.

But in the meantime he was a sitting duck. He needed help. And there was only one person who might believe him, one person who might be able to help him pull off his plan.

He hurried to the back door and rapped on it. When Officer Jim whisked back the curtain from the door's tiny, head-high window, Larry almost didn't recognize him. His jaw was scruffy, his blonde crewcut had grown out and was starting to flop. A splotch of red joined the pale blue of his right eye, the skin around that socket puffy and yellowish, a shiner not yet healed. Larry felt a stab of panic. Officer Jim might not be up to what he had in mind.

Officer Jim opened the door a crack, showing his black slippers and a ratty, red-and-gray checked bathrobe that descended to his bare calves. "What do you want?"

"I want to talk to you about the Hellers."

Officer Jim looked past Larry, his eyes jittery, his gaze sweeping across the backyard. He grunted, and opened the door wider. Larry stepped inside. Officer Jim shut and locked the door, then gestured toward a chair at the kitchen table.

As Larry sat, Officer Jim limped over and eased himself down into a chair catercorner from Larry's. A blackened frying pan and a sauce pan three-quarters full of greasy water sat on the stove. Stacks of crusty plates and glasses filled both sinks. A loaf of white bread, its wrapper left open, a saucer holding a gouged and melted stick of butter, and a haphazard pile of newspapers and junk mail cluttered the countertop. The sports page was open on the kitchen table, a plate littered with crumbs and an empty coffee mug on top of the paper. Larry felt no need to ask if anybody else was there. He said, "I didn't come here to bullshit you. I was ... I am supplying the Hellers with pot."

Officer Jim puffed out his cheeks, then exhaled. "Why are you telling me this? The department's off your back. You can do whatever you want."

"You and I both know that it wasn't some out-of-towners that hurt you. You and I both know that I don't have any out-of-town muscle. You and I both know why you can't tell the truth about what really happened."

Officer Jim closed his eyes. His shoulders slumped. "I don't wanna get into this again."

"C'mon. We both know I told the truth about giant squirrels attacking Mrs. Reeves. The night before, I told Meryl Heller about Reeves, about how she was drowning regular squirrels. The next morning the giant ones attacked her. Then they attacked me, because of some hard feelings some of the Hellers have towards me. I know it was giant squirrels that attacked you, because you were a threat to the Hellers' weed connection. I told them that you were making me leave town."

Officer Jim opened his eyes. "So you're telling me that these giant squirrels and the Hellers are connected. That the Hellers can sic them on people."

Larry swallowed. He braced himself. "The Hellers are the giant squirrels." He sat there and endured Officer Jim's scrutiny. When he was sure that Officer Jim believed that he was serious, he didn't give Officer Jim a chance to call him 'crazy.' "Think about how they attacked you. I bet it was a trap like humans would set. I bet it was a trap like no animal in the history of animals ever set." He took a breath. "I'm not asking you to believe me. I'm asking you to help me prove it to you."

"How in the world are you gonna do that?"

"We catch one of them and make him change. I'm thinking Slappy. We make him tell us everything."

Officer Jim chewed it over. "Then what?"

It was Larry's turn to scrutinize Officer Jim. He hadn't expected him to be so reasonable. He didn't detect any signs of mockery on the cop's face. He licked his lips. "You help me catch Slappy. We'll make him change and record it. On videotape. Then we'll make him confess and tape that too. We'll make him tell us everything. Then we'll turn him loose, tell him to tell the rest of them that if anything happens to us, copies of the tape will go out to every tabloid and every television station we can think of, and there won't be any place for them to hide. It will be all over for them."

"So your plan is to kidnap Slappy, coerce a confession out of him, then blackmail the Hellers."

"I don't see any other way. I think that Mike and Bill know that I know the truth about them, but they didn't kill me, because I'm useful to them. Thank God I never gave them my connection like I was gonna, or they probably would've killed me, and I'd be buried out in a cornfield somewhere. And I bet they kept this little fact to themselves, or Casey and his stooges would really have a reason to come after me. But I overheard Casey and them talking, they're just waiting for things to cool down before they *do* come after me. They mean to kill me."

"Every cop I know has tried to catch Slappy, but he's still out there, running free. If we try to catch him and he gets away, then what? They'll know we're up to something, and they'll come after the both of us. Then what? We supposed to team up and go out and hunt them down? Get them before they get us?"

Larry shook his head. "It won't come to that. Slappy trusts me. I'm sure I can lure him into a trap."

Officer Jim sighed, looked past Larry, and said, "Why are you telling me this bullshit? This crap doesn't have nothing to do with me."

"But they jumped you!"

Officer Jim, with a grimace, rose from his chair. He looked down on Larry. "It was Rockford goons that jumped me. If I were you, I'd get the fuck out of town. Now I gotta go soak in the tub, doctor's orders, so get the fuck out of my house."

"But ..."

Officer Jim pulled a small, snub-nosed handgun out of his robe's pocket and aimed it at Larry. "Get up." Larry did. Officer Jim used the gun to gesture towards the door.

Larry, outside on the patio, turned around and looked at Officer Jim. "But you believe me, right?

"Don't come around here anymore." Officer Jim slammed the door in Larry's face.

Chapter Twenty-two

Larry hunkered down in the tall grass but kept his eyes trained on the treetops. The high-noon sunshine glared through the hole in the canopy and beat down on the small clearing. He slid his palm across his slick forehead and wicked away the sweat, brushing a hank of longish bangs to the side of the head. The cool shade surrounding the clearing beckoned to him, but he couldn't bring himself to abandon open sky for the dark green overhang.

His fists throbbed. He uncurled his fingers and rubbed his hands together. There was nowhere else but the Weeds where he could pull it off. Last night, after Officer Jim slammed the door in his face, he'd hung up three times before the right dude answered the phone.

A swishing drew his attention to the direction of the riverside path. When the racket indicated a carefree pace, a *human* pace, Larry rose to his full height and called out, "Over here!"

Be cool, be cool ...

His stomach acids fizzed as his visitor crashed through the bushes and into the clearing. The bill of his greasy ballcap skewed low and shadowed his eyes and nose, but the fringe of stringy brown hair and the goatish chin-whiskers, and the black Iron Maiden tee shirt and the faded jeans flapping on the stunted, scrawny frame, left no doubt. A spicy sinsemilla aroma unfurled from Slappy.

Larry's chest tightened while shaking hands with Slappy, whose eyelids sagged so low that they covered half his pupils. Red jags brambled the visible whites of his eyes. Slappy was already stoned out of his gourd. *Good.*

A goofy grin stretched Slappy's lips. Larry's return smile felt rigid, so he showed his teeth, and that felt worse, but Slappy didn't seem to notice anything, didn't give any tells that he knew that Larry knew, didn't give any tells that he was pretending not to know that Larry knew. Still, face to face, that sizzle and pock echoed in Larry's skull, and he barely managed to suppress a flinch.

"So what's up, man?" Slappy asked.

Larry produced a joint. "You wanna catch one?"

Slappy smiled wider. "Sure."

Larry gestured toward a downed trunk and a nearby stump in the center of the clearing. Slappy took the stump. Larry tottered behind on his stiff legs, then hopped up and settled on the trunk. He lit the joint and passed it to Slappy.

Larry wiped the fresh sweat off his forehead and tried not to look at the weeds that hid the rope. In his mind, he ran through the move for the umpteenth time. He had to be crisp. He knew he could overpower Slappy, but he also knew how fast Slappy could change, and if that happened, then all bets were off.

Slappy handed the smoking joint to Larry, then said, "So what's this all about?"

Larry cleared the sludge from his throat. He'd prepared a couple legitimate remarks. "Why the hell didn't anybody tell me that Meryl's fourteen?"

Slappy reddened. "She made us swear not to."

Larry realized that he was scrutinizing Slappy's face for squirrelish features. He twitched back. "Why?" He took a shallow hit off the joint.

"I s'pose she thought you guys might have a chance."

"How? What did she think was gonna happen when I found out?" Larry reached the joint to Slappy.

Slappy shook his head. "I dunno man. You're gonna have'ta ask her."

"Fair enough. I just wish somebody would've said something." He rubbed his clammy palms together, working up little black rollers of filth. "Anyways, what I really wanna talk about is Casey."

Slappy nodded. "Caught everybody off guard. Nobody knew he was getting out so early. Some weird technicality cut his time short."

Larry watched him take a deep drag. *Good.* The more stoned he got, the slower his reactions would be. Larry had the opposite problem. He'd overdosed on caffeine this morning. Sitting still, maintaining a semblance of stoner mellowness, only cranked him up more. He couldn't understand how he could sweat so much while his mouth was bone dry. He worked his tongue around his gums to dredge up some moisture, then said, "He wants to kick my ass."

Slappy, his lungs full of smoke, wisps escaping his lips as he spoke in a breathless voice, said, "Yeah, 'cause of Meryl."

116

"Seems like it's more than that."

Slappy passed the joint, exhaled a tremendous cloud, then said, "There's some shit between Casey and Mike."

"Like who's gonna be the boss."

Slappy's dope-slacked features straightened just a bit. Larry took another shallow hit, holding most of the smoke in his mouth. Slappy said, "Something like that, yeah. Thing is, Casey probably would'a come after you 'cause of Meryl, no matter what." Slappy's tone pitched a little brittle, saying, "He knows about you and Margaret."

Larry exhaled. "I meant to clear everything up at the party. Things just got out of hand."

Slappy sighed. "I don't blame you. If I had a shot at Margaret, I'd do the same thing."

"Looks like I might've blown it with her anyways." Larry winced. He didn't like to think it, much less say it out loud. He sniffed, then said, "Anyways, this thing with Casey, it's a problem."

Slappy waved off Larry's extension of the joint, which was now on the roachy side. Slappy stood up and swayed. "Whoa, headrush." He gave himself a couple light slaps to the cheek. "Lemme take a whiz, then we'll figure it out."

Larry nodded. Slappy shoved his way into the tall weeds. The lush green swallowed him. Larry stopped himself with the joint halfway to his lips, a reflex action. He stubbed it out. He'd make his move when Slappy came back. He stood, shook out his legs, then resettled on the trunk. He lit a cigarette. *Good.* He'd look casual, and he'd wait till Slappy sat back down, then he'd strike.

Slappy re-emerged from a different point in the brush. Larry's breath hitched. Slappy stumbled, then righted himself. He guffawed. "Whoa. Got lost. Dude, I'm so wasted." He frowned at the ground, stooped, and hauled up a section of rough rope. "What's this doing here?"

Larry stammered. He urged himself to get off his ass, but his legs seemed paralyzed. Slappy yanked on the rope, which flicked up from the low scrub and tautened, revealing one end cinched around a nearby tree. Slappy yanked the other way and caught the free end as it whipped toward him. The noose, a shorter piece of rope tied crosswise a little below and each of its ends terminating in wrist-sized slipknots, dangled from Slappy's hands. Slappy gawked at his discovery, then his head did a slow rise upward, his eyes wide, the corners of his mouth downsloped, the full realization written all over his face.

Larry threw himself at Slappy. His fingertips grazed Slappy's back. Low branches smacked the cap from Slappy's head. The rope tangled Larry's feet. Slappy flailed into the trees. Larry dove forward and snatched Slappy's ankle. Slappy kicked, dragged Larry on his belly, then shucked his dirty sneaker and his dirtier sock, and crashed into the weeds. Larry tried to get up but his balky knee gave and he crumpled back to the dirt. He cradled his head. He sobbed, "*Fuck!*"

Chapter Twenty-three

Larry watched the numbers flip on the pump's meter. He wished he'd been smart enough to fill up the Olds before meeting with Slappy. At least Slappy was on foot, so he had a little breathing room before the rest of the Hellers found out. Still, he'd feel a helluva lot better once he was heading west down the highway, putting Murray behind himself for good.

He eyed the beat-up blue LTD that crossed the highway and cruised north down McKinley. From the shotgun seat, the glare of the westering sun glinted off of a pair of mirrored shades. He decided that the gas tank was full enough. He pulled out the nozzle and hung it up, then hurried inside and paid. By the time he had the Olds on the highway, the LTD was speeding back up McKinley.

He floored it. He'd risk a speeding ticket if it meant Casey had to explain to a trooper why he was speeding too. He glanced in the rearview mirror. The LTD followed a ways behind him. The road ahead curved empty and slow into the west. Occasional farmsteads broke up the tall sun-faded green of the corn.

Larry zipped by a yellow road sign warning of an approaching S-curve. He had to brake. He damned himself for taking an unfamiliar route as Casey came roaring up on his ass. Bumper-to-bumper they whipped through the S-curve.

They accelerated into a straightaway, and Larry was ready to open it up, but he spotted a cluster of houses lining both sides of the road. A green sign posted the speed limit at forty-five, another posted the name of the township as Lightsville, population 80.

Larry slammed his right hand against the steering wheel. He slowed the Olds. Casey rode Larry's ass so close that his brutal smirk reflected in Larry's rearview.

In less than a minute they cleared Lightsville. The highway ahead spanned empty to the horizon. Larry stomped the gas pedal. The LTD veered into the oncoming lane and pulled abreast. The Olds began to rattle. He glanced over and saw Bill scrambling over the front seat into the back. Casey whipped the wheel and the LTD banged into the Olds.

119

Larry screamed and took his foot off the gas and almost jammed down the brake, then his world spooled. His hands lost the wheel. Something smacked him in the temple and his field of vision flared white. The Olds jerked to a halt. His eyelids fluttered. Everything was green, and the steering wheel was gone. A moment later he processed that the green was corn and that he was sitting in the passenger seat.

His head ached. He touched the pulsing spot below his temple and winced. His fingers came back smudged with blood. He glanced up, his eyes seeking the rearview, but the mirror was gone. He closed his eyes and breathed deep. Far off, a crow cawed. The breeze soughed through corn tassels. Nearby, a car door slammed.

Larry's eyes snapped open. He fumbled with the handle then shoved the door open. He stumbled out of the car. He reeled, staring at the swath that the Olds had cut through the corn. The road seemed a long ways down the snaking strip of mowed-down cornstalks. He shook his head, trying to refocus his vision. He had a hunting knife in the trunk. He walked all the way to the trunk before he realized the keys were still in the ignition.

He sensed the clock ticking. Casey would have weapons at the ready, baseball bats, knives, maybe guns. He used the car to prop himself up while he worked himself around to the driver's side. He leaned in the window and grabbed for the keys. He couldn't jiggle them loose.

"Hey, fella."

The reedy voice startled Larry. He straightened up and smacked the back of his head against the interior's roof.

"You okay?"

Larry extracted himself from the car and saw a thin old man wearing a conductor's hat and bib-overalls over a plaid shirt. The old man's head quivered, and he took painstaking steps, as if he was terrified of falling.

Larry's voice sounded muffled to himself when he said, "They ran me off the road."

"I saw that. Ope, you got a gash on your noggin."

Larry touched the sticky, warm spot on his forehead above his left eye.

"Let's work on gettin' you up to the road."

"They tried ..." Larry swooned, then plummeted butt-first onto crushed cornstalks.

"Shit on a biscuit."

Larry sat there while the old man examined his wounded head. Larry watched the world swirl and shimmy. He strove to guide things back to their rightful places.

"It don't look too bad," the old man said. "Can you get up?"

"Yeah."

Larry flattened his palms against the downed cornstalks and tried to push himself up. The old man grabbed him under the arms and hauled Larry to his feet. Larry thought the old man was a lot stronger than he looked.

The old man draped Larry's arm around his neck, staggered under the burden, then stabilized himself, saying, "There we go, upsy-daisy. One foot after the other." He began to walk Larry towards the road. "We'll get you to the hospital. Tractor'll pull your car right up to the road. How's that sound?"

"Thank you. They ran me off."

"You boy's drag racing?"

Larry shook his head. "Where are they?"

"Your buddies? They shot over the hill like a bat out of Hell. Lost sight of 'em."

"I'm right here, Joe."

The old man blurted, "Jesus H. Christ!" He turned around, taking Larry with him. Casey emerged from the standing corn, leveling a pistol at them. "Casey Heller."

"Sorry Joe," Casey said. "Didn't mean for you to get messed up in this." Casey pulled the trigger. The old man, Joe, jerked, Larry feeling the tremor though his own body. Joe groaned and doubled over. Larry slipped off of Joe's shoulder and dropped to his knees.

Casey jabbed the gun's barrel toward Larry. "See what you made me do? Old Joe here never hurt anybody, and you made me go and kill him."

"No."

"Yes you did. Ain't my fault, that's for sure."

Larry raised his head. Casey aimed the gun between Larry's eyes. Larry said, "You're not gonna get away with this."

"Quit your bitchin', and come take your medicine. You drove right out in the middle of nowhere, so ain't nobody gonna hear a damned thing. Just hold still now."

Larry closed his eyes. He wished he could put up a better fight, but his limbs felt too heavy. The gunshot made him jump. He didn't feel any fresh pain.

Casey shouted, "God damn it, Joe!"

Larry opened his eyes. Joe's arms embraced Casey's calves. Casey pointed the gun straight down at Joe and opened fire. Larry cringed at each blast. The gun clicked empty. Joe's arms relaxed from Casey's legs and he spasmed at Casey's feet.

Casey threw his head back and screamed, "Fuck!"

Joe's arm flopped, then he stilled.

Casey glowered at Joe's body. "Look what you made me do." He raised his foot and stomped his big black boot into the middle of Joe's bloody back. Casey took a step back and kicked Joe's head.

Larry closed his eyes. He couldn't watch this, but he could hear it, as Casey went berserk, kicking and stomping Joe's corpse while growling curses. Finally Casey's rage deflated into ragged panting.

Larry opened his eyes. Casey was leaning on his knees and glaring at him, the gun in his right hand. Casey said, "Used up all my bullets. Guess we're gonna have to do this the hard way."

Casey took a step towards Larry. He stopped and regarded the gun. "Gonna put this in your hand when I'm done, and make it look like you killed ol' Joe."

"You're a moron."

Casey clicked his teeth together, then lashed forward, clocking Larry in the jaw with his left fist. The blow spun Larry to the dirt. Casey howled.

Larry turned his head and opened his eyes. His vision was blurry, but he could make out Casey cradling his injured fist. It hurt Larry's jaw to laugh, and to speak, yet he endured both while saying, "You really are a moron."

Casey seethed. "No more fuckin' around." He threw the gun down and swarmed over Larry, who tried to fight back, but Casey was too strong. Casey flipped Larry onto his back, then squatted on his chest, his knees pinning Larry's shoulders. Larry flashbacked to the Hellers' party, when Casey had tried this same maneuver, when Mike had come barreling out of nowhere to save Larry from having his face caved in. Larry scrunched his eyes shut in anticipation of a hail of blows.

He *hurked* when Casey's hands clamped around his throat. He opened his eyes and wheezed. Casey's lank brown hair hung down and swung with Larry's convulsions. A thick vein, in the shape of a lightning bolt, bulged and throbbed under the skin of Casey's forehead. His eyes were slits, his crooked yellow teeth bared, a string of spittle drooled from his lower lip.

Panic drove Larry into wilder gyrations, but he couldn't throw Casey, couldn't even free an arm. The strength drained from his muscles, and along with it the energy to fuel his panic.

He floundered towards clarity. He swung his knee upward, but Casey was too far forward, and when his kneecap bumped Casey's kidney, Casey didn't budge. Instead, Casey worked his thumbs around to Larry's Adam's apple and pressed down.

Larry wormed his shoulders lower and freed his elbows. He beat at Casey's back, then hooked his hand's into Casey's belt, and yanked Casey backwards. Casey wobbled, his grip wavered, and Larry stole some air before Casey was able to resettle and to reassert his chokehold.

Casey murmured, "Stay still, you slippery mothafucka."

Larry tugged on Casey's belt with all his might. Casey leaned forward against Larry's effort. He barked a harsh laugh. "I can hold out longer than you can. Give it up. Hey, You're goin' all purple, did you know that?"

Larry mustered one last do-or-die yank on Casey's belt. Casey elevated to counter, and created a small gap between his crotch and Larry's stomach. Larry jammed his right hand in between, palm up. Casey bore down with his ass, trying to stop the progress of Larry's hand. Dealing with this threat distracted Casey from his chokehold, allowing Larry to suck in more air. Larry stabbed his hand a little further. His fingers dug into the taut denim covering Casey's crotch. He didn't know if he had reached the critical place, not until he squeezed and Casey yelped.

Casey released Larry's neck. Larry filled his lungs before Casey smacked him across the jaw. He squeezed harder and Casey drove his hands between his legs. Screeching, Casey broke Larry's grip and rolled away.

Larry flipped over on his belly and pushed himself up to his hands and knees, all the while gasping in giant breaths.

Casey moaned. "You mothafucka!. I'll kill you, you mothafucka!" He punted Larry in the stomach, knocking the wind right back out of him. As Larry tried to roll away, Casey yelled, "I'm gonna kick the shit out'a you, and then I'm gonna kill you!"

"Just do it and get it the fuck over with!" Barney said.

"You take care of it?" Casey said.

"Yeah. So just do it, and get it over … wait!"

Larry stopped crawling. The hum of a car motoring along the highway grew louder from the west. The Hellers ducked down. Larry stood up, but the field was a good eight feet lower than the road. He screamed as the car whizzed by. He tottered off towards the road, but one of them tackled him from behind, the two of them going down and taking more cornstalks with them. The car didn't slow.

"It's clear," Barney said. "Do it!"

Casey held Larry down. Larry squirmed, but Casey managed to stay on top. Casey called out to Barney, "Hey asshole, I'm out'a bullets. You think it's easy to kill a man with your bare hands? Why don't get the fuck over here and help me!"

Casey kept Larry on his belly. He told Barney, "I got an idea." He directed Barney to sit on Larry's legs and to seize Larry's wrists. Barney leaned back and wishboned Larry. Casey lowered himself into the gap between Barney and Larry's arms and kneeled on the middle of Larry's back. Larry could barely move.

"Okay," Casey said. "Just hold him tight, this could take a little while. It ain't like on TV."

Larry recognized the clinking as Casey unbuckling his belt.

"Lift up your head now, man," Cased said. "This will be over before you know it."

Larry smushed his forehead to the ground as hard as he could, preventing Casey from slipping the belt over his head.

"Got a lotta fight in him," Casey said. "Gotta give him that."

"Fuck," Barney said. "Just hurry the fuck up and do it!"

Casey wrapped his fist in Larry's hair and drew Larry's head back. Larry's scream mutated into a growl as, with his neck muscles alone, he tugged back a few inches.

Casey began to work the noose over the fist tangled in Larry's hair, then he said, "That's not gonna work."

"Will you quit fuckin' around!" Barney said. "Somebody's bound to see the fence and the corn, and come lookin'!"

Casey shouted, "I'm tryin' my best! Just shut the fuck up!"

Casey let go of Larry's hair. Larry pressed his forehead to the dirt and the broken stalks. He twisted his neck and saw Casey putting his right arm through the loop. Larry moaned. He tried to wrest his arms free from Barney, but the little bastard held on tight.

"Okay," Casey said, "I got it figured out." Using his right hand, he grabbed Larry's hair again, and tugged his head away from the dirt. He used his left hand to work the looped belt down his right forearm. The belt scraped Larry's forehead. "Pretty slick, eh?"

Casey edged the loop down. When the loop reached the bridge of Larry's nose, he strained outward, and snagged the belt. Casey reached down to unhook the loop. Larry lunged his mouth at Casey's left hand, his teeth tearing into the meaty part of Casey's palm.

Casey shrieked. He yanked Larry by the hair, but Larry bit harder, his teeth sinking deeper. Casey continued to shriek. He released Larry's hair and clubbed Larry on the top of his head. The blow broke Larry's hold on Casey's hand.

Larry's head rebounded off the dirt, and he spat out a bloody, ragged chunk of Casey's palm. He was free. He turned his head and saw Casey, sitting among the broken cornstalks, shivering, with blood gouting between the fingers of his right hand, which was clamped over his mutilated left. Barney scrambled towards Casey.

Larry weaved upright. He plunged into the corn. He swatted stalks out of his way. Soon he could see the grassy ditch, just rows ahead. He burst out of the corn and flipped over the barbwire fence. His face whapped into the grass nose-first. The barbs caught in his jeans and held. He bobbed up and down, the top wire suspending his hips.

Dazed, blood streaming from his nostrils, he managed to rip himself free. He crawled up the side of the ditch. He scrabbled to his feet on the graveled shoulder of the highway. There were no cars in sight, not even the farmer's, or the LTD.

He turned and looked back the way he'd come. Corn tassels shook, marking their progress towards him. He started running towards town.

At first all he heard was his own labored breathing and the slaps of his soles on the pavement. Too soon, another set of footfalls joined his, then another. He scanned the horizon. No houses, no cars, just corn. He glanced over his shoulder. Casey was bare-chested, his blood-soaked shirt wadded around his damaged hand. Barney was several yards behind Casey, whose long strides ate up Larry's lead.

Larry knew he wasn't gonna make it. He was too battered, he had spent too much energy just getting this far. He would've stopped and slugged it out, but he couldn't fight the two of them. Casey closed the gap, Larry judging Casey's position by his gasps. Larry ground his teeth. He had to fight them. Maybe he could hold them off until a car came. The barbwire fence flickered through this mind.

He slowed, breathing deep and fast, gathering as much strength as he had left. He felt Casey's fingertips brush his shoulder. He dropped to his knees. He bent down as far as he could, arching his back, touching his brow to the pavement, and he laced his fingers behind his head. Casey's shins slammed into his ass. Casey's body levered over him, followed by a violent, hollow *thock*. Larry thought of aluminum bats smashing into Halloween pumpkins.

Barney screamed, "Casey!"

One of Casey's legs, still draped over Larry's back, shuddered and flipped off of him. Barney's soles slapped against the blacktop. He raised his head. Barney knelt by Casey, who lied face down on the road. A small pool of blood spread out from under Casey's face.

Larry stood. Barney tried to rouse Casey. Larry had some of his breath back by the time Barney looked up at him. Somewhere along the way Barney had lost his mirrored shades. For a second Larry forgot about everything and gaped at Barney's monstrous right eye, which was easily twice the size as the left, and eyeball itself a bulging white hemisphere with no apparent iris and a black pinprick for a pupil. Yellowish pus oozed from its tear duct.

Barney blinked, and the right eyelid gummed shut a little longer than the left, then slid up sludgy-slow. Larry grimaced. Barney said, "You killed him."

Larry assumed a fighting stance. Barney rose to his feet. Larry looked past Barney. A vehicle had broken the eastern horizon. "Somebody's coming."

Barney didn't move. "You're gonna go to prison for this."

Larry didn't think so. He squinted. The vehicle's back end wobbled. The laboring engine sputtered. Barney turned to look. He uttered a dry chuckle.

Larry spotted Mike Heller behind camper's steering wheel.

Chapter Twenty-four

The decrepit orange and white camper pulled over to the side of the road. Mike stepped outside, Bill jumped out of the shotgun seat. Hellers poured out of the backend. Larry recognized Looey, Jackie, Jay-Jay, and Slappy. The other two Larry'd never seen before, but their stunted statures and long brown hair, as well as their jeans and black tee shirts emblazoned with the splashy logos of heavy metal bands, marked them as Heller Boys.

Mike walked up and took one look at Casey lying facedown in the middle of the highway, then hollered, "All right. Let's clean it up."

The other Hellers circled around and gawked at Casey. Slappy shot Larry a dirty look. Mike started barking out specific orders. Slappy took off into the corn, following the swath the Olds had cut through the field. Jackie and Jay-Jay, and the unknown Hellers, picked up Casey, each hoisting a limb, and trundled him to the rear of the camper. Mike, after taking Barney aside and whispering to him, sent Looey scampering west down the highway. Bill put an arm around Barney's shoulders and started walking him to the back of the camper. Barney, fuming, shoved Bill's arm away and stalked ahead by himself.

Larry turned away from the pool of blood staining the road. Mike approached him, and, his features placid, said, "Just hang loose a minute."

Larry hobbled to the road's shoulder and sat down with his back to the busy Hellers. He closed his eyes and bowed his head. He wished for a car to come, police would be a miracle. He listened to Hellers rushing into the corn on the other side of the road. Going after that farmer's body, he supposed. Casey deserved to die for murdering that poor old guy. Besides that, it was self-defense. Larry searched himself, but he didn't feel any different, except for the pings and aches of his newest rash of injuries, the jaw, the kidney, the bumps and bruises from the crash, his throat …

From the west a car sped towards them. He opened his eyes and turned his head. The LTD screeched to a halt a few feet in front of the camper.

Mike pulled Larry to his feet and helped him into the LTD's passenger seat. Mike took the wheel, then brought the LTD up to the legal speed limit and kept it there. He flicked on the radio and turned up the volume. He drummed his fingers on the steering wheel to the tail end of ZZ Top's *La Grange*. Larry took a sidelong look at Mike, and he could've sworn that Mike was trying not to smile.

At the song's end a jeweler's commercial took over. Mike turned the volume down and said, "Don't be so glum, chum. The boys'll clean up the mess, and nobody'll be the wiser. Hell, they'll even bring back your Olds. Can't say what shape it'll be in …"

"You're not gonna kill me?"

Mike chuckled. "I think we got enough dead bodies to deal with for one day." He sighed. "I guess things've gotten a little nuts. Can't fuck it up now, or the whole thing might come down on our heads."

They didn't speak as they passed through Lightsville, then Larry said, "Where we going?"

"Guess this all seems pretty crazy to you."

Larry snorted. "Crazy?" He surprised himself by mustering up some sarcasm while saying, "Nahhh. What's the big deal? You guys are a bunch of weresquirrels. What's crazy about that?"

Mike sucked his teeth. "We don't like that word. *I* don't like your tone."

Larry's bravado vanished. He hugged himself.

Mike chuckled. "Relax, man." He slapped Larry on the knee. Larry jerked, pressed closer to the door, thought about jumping for it. Mike said, "You're my main man, my connection. I'm not gonna let anything happen to you. So please don't try to jump out of the car. You're banged up enough as it is. And we'd catch ya anyways."

Larry shifted away from the door. "I was bit. Oh god … am I gonna turn into one?"

"It don't work that way. Now listen up, I'm not gonna play Twenty Questions with you. All you need to know is that I own you now."

"What?"

"Let's see, murder, drug dealing, statutory rape … that's just off the top of my head. You're gonna do what I say from now on."

"No."

"Chill, man. I'm not gonna make you give me your connect. But no more of this running-away bullshit. We got eyes everywhere, and we will find you. Anyways, don't you got a court date to keep?"

Larry muttered, "Why are you doing this to me?"

Mike laughed. "I'm protecting you. But you're probably gonna need a new place to live. We're not done with that fucking old bitch. Not by a long shot."

Mike slowed the LTD and steered it onto a gravel road.

"Where are we going?" Larry asked.

"My place." Before Larry could ask what for, Mike said, "Great tune!" He cranked up the volume on Led Zeppelin's *Kashmir*. The next song, *Voodoo Chile*, by Jimi Hendrix, was into the first chorus when they pulled up in front of Mike's house.

Mike killed the engine but turned the key over to battery mode. They sat there and listened to the song all the way to the end, then Mike switched the radio off and said, "Follow me." He got out of the car and started walking towards the barns.

Larry got out of the car and stood still.

Mike looked back and smiled. "Don't worry, I'm not taking you out back to put you out of your misery. We got some work to do, so hop to it."

Larry limped after Mike. The pain from his left knee began to overshadow his other wounds. Mike went into a barn and came out with two wooden-handled spades. He handed one to Larry and said, "We got some holes to dig."

"What?"

"Hey, you killed him, you bury him. Them's the rules." Mike gave Larry a worn pair of brown cotton work-gloves and led him beyond the last barn. Mike stopped on a patch of dirt between the barn and the corn. "This is good. Used to be a garden here, so the soil's already been turned once or twice. Should be an easy dig."

A few hardy weeds sprung knee-high from the gray dirt. Larry speared the spade into the soil. The blade bonged metallic while throwing up a few thin chips.

Mike shrugged. "Might be a little hard-packed and stony on top."

They dug in silence. The going was easier a couple inches down. When they heard the sputter of the camper's engine, Mike said, "Keep digging. I'll be right back."

130

Larry took a break. His grave was deeper than Mike's anyways. Now that the rest of them were back, they'd be finished before sunset.

He started digging again when he heard their approaching voices.

Mike directed Slappy, Jackie, and the two unknown Hellers graveside. The four of them toted a corpse swaddled in an old blue blanket, which they dropped to the ground, the impact creating a solid *thud*. Larry guessed that was the corpse of the farmer. Jackie glared at Larry as the four Hellers headed back for the other corpse.

Mike went so far as to pick up the free spade, but then he just leaned on it and looked over the holes, and the mounds of loose dirt beside the holes.

"What about coffins?" Larry asked.

Mike smirked. "This ain't a service. This is hiding bodies. We don't wanna make it any harder on the worms than we have to."

Larry dug up a few more spadefuls of dirt. The four returned bearing another corpse, this one wrapped in a snot-green blanket. They placed the corpse next to the shallower grave, the one Mike had been digging. They didn't seem to notice when the left arm flipped out of the blanket, showing Casey's mangled left palm.

Larry turned away and dug. Mike said, "I'll check on ya in a bit."

Their footsteps receded toward the house. Soon after, death metal, some band Larry had never heard before, destroyed the calm. Larry dug, wondering how deep he was supposed to go, wondering if they were watching him from the field. The sun went down. A little later, Mike, stinking of cheap beer and reefer, brought Larry a Coleman lantern. He inspected Larry's work, Larry now toiling in the grave that Mike had begun. He said, "Won't be much longer," then he strolled back to the house, which still raged with anonymous satanic metal.

Despite the gloves, blisters mushroomed on Larry's palms. Each new shovelful of dirt seemed heavier than the last. His belly felt hollow, his lips cracked. His back hurt worse than his knee. He stopped. This second grave was now chest deep, like the first. He leaned on the shovel and bowed until he forehead rested on the shovel's handle. He thought he could fall asleep on his feet. The sound of light footfalls brought his head back up. Meryl followed

131

Mike. Canvass sneakers, loose blue jeans, and a baggy white tee shirt, she wore more clothes than Larry had ever seen her in before, and with her hair pulled back in a stubby ponytail, she looked like a kid. Larry felt sick to his stomach.

She carried a brown plastic pitcher, Mike held a pair of jelly jars. He said, "Go on and say it if you gotta."

Meryl handed the pitcher to Mike. She stared at the ground and said, "Thank you." Then she hurried back toward the house.

Larry peered up at Mike. "What was that all about?"

Mike inspected the graves. "I think they're deep enough." He set the pitcher on the ground next to the grave Larry was standing in, then sat down, dangling his legs over the ledge. He handed a jelly jar to Larry and said, "You must be fucking thirsty."

Larry held the jar while Mike poured ice cold lemonade from the pitcher. Larry guzzled the jar empty before Mike could fill his own. The lemonade made Larry's chest tingle.

While Mike filled his jar again, Larry said, "Why did she say that?"

Mike looked Larry in the eyes. He shrugged, then said, "I guess it won't hurt to tell. You know all our other secrets. Casey used to … well, you know. And he treated her kind of rough."

"He molested her?"

Mike nodded. "On a regular basis."

"Why didn't you stop him?"

"Gotta pick your battles. In case you didn't notice, Casey used to be a kind of a badass." Mike stood and walked over to Casey's corpse. He nudged it with his boot. "The truth is, he was a motherfucker. Made my life a living hell, until I was big enough to fight back. Plus, he always had Barney and them on his side." He sighed, then finished off his lemonade and set the jelly jar on the ground. "C'mon. Give me a hand."

They heaved the corpses into the graves. They shoveled dirt back into the holes. With the two of them working, the job flew by. Mike, while tamping down the fresh mound, said, "It's definitely for the best." He slung his spade over his shoulder. "But you got one last problem. Barney wants to fight you to the death."

"I figured. And if I get past him, then I gotta deal with Jackie, then Jay-Jay, and who knows who else. It'll never end."

"Nah, I can handle Jacko and them, but Barney, he's got a legitimate beef. Now, it might not be the worst thing in the world if you killed him too …"

Larry shook his head. "I'm not gonna kill him."

Mike chuckled. "You're not hearing me. Either you kill him, or he kills you. Barney's got rights. We do things our own way. He's demanded a death match."

"What the fuck?"

"He demanded it, and we voted on it, and well, it's been decided that he has cause. But don't worry about it. While you've been digging these graves, he's been getting drunker than a skunk. He's blitzed. Now's the *perfect* time."

"Are you nuts? I've been in a car accident. I've had the shit kicked out of me. I've been digging for hours. I can barely lift my fucking arms."

"It's been decided. Nothing I can do about it now. It's already started, by the way. Goes until one of you is dead." Mike headed back for the house.

"Wait!"

Mike called out, "I can't interfere."

Larry watched him disappear among the barns. He whipped his head from side to side. He gripped his shovel. He spotted the pitcher, grabbed it, brought it to his lips and drained the dregs of the lemonade. He doused the lantern. From the south he heard rustling in the corn. Maybe Barney in squirrel form. He dashed north into the corn. He held the shovel so that the blade was near his head. He was ready to brain the first thing he saw.

Chapter Twenty-five

Larry's right calf cramped. He yelped and surged down to massage the compacted muscle. Tears seeped from his clenched eyelids. His aching shoulders and forearms flagged. One of the blisters dotting the pads of his palms burst and burned. He lurched up from the chair and limped around the kitchen table, finally walking off the cramp. He sagged back into the chair. His groan abraded his raw throat, Casey's bruising chokehold leaving behind a mottling of blue and yellow finger-marks, and his groan reawakened the throbbing in his jaw, still swollen where Casey clocked him. After yesterday, the crash, the assault and battery, the grave digging, and the frantic bolt home, he couldn't fight Barney if he wanted to, even if Barney shocked the hell out of him and came at him one-on-one, man-to-man.

He had to make a break for it.

He laid his pounding forehead in his hands, careful to avoid compressing the blisters. When he looked outside this morning, the Olds, a little dinged up, sat in its usual spot beside the curb. The engine wouldn't turn over, stolen distributor cap, sugar in the gas tank, he'd been too beat up and exhausted to check. For good measure, they'd cleaned out the trunk, his stuff, his stash, his money, all gone. He didn't have enough cash in his wallet for a bus ticket, and he was out of cigarettes. He had to work his shift today, and hope his tips put him over the top.

He took a sip of his lukewarm coffee. If his tips didn't bridge the gap, he'd have to stick around another day, and that would give Barney more chances at him. The walk to and from work. He knew he wouldn't sleep at night, not with Barney creeping around the treetops, maybe sneaking into the house through the roof. It wasn't fair. It was self-defense. And Casey was a murderer, had gunned down that farmer just for being in the wrong place at the wrong time. Larry eyed the clock built into the stove. He could crawl back into bed, get a couple hours of sleep before work. Barney wouldn't dare attack in broad daylight. But Casey hadn't thought twice about killing that farmer. He doubted Mike would think twice about siccing the rest of them on Mrs. Reeves. He had to warn her.

The porch's screen door whinged open and shut. He sighed. He'd been waiting for her to come in from the garden. The other boarders were gone to work. Now was the perfect time. His heartbeat accelerated, his stomach went cold, despite the blue warmth suffusing through the spotless windows over the sinks. Like an itch he couldn't scratch, there was a way to tell her so that she'd believe, he knew it, but he couldn't reach it.

Mrs. Reeves shuffled into the kitchen, her gait still a little slower than before the attack, but her customary gardening uniform, the white sneakers, the high-wasted khakis, and the long-sleeved, flower-print blouse, snapped sharp and pristine. She took off her brand-new black wraparounds and said, "My Lord. What happened to you?"

He cinched the flaps of his robes shut over his chest. "Sit down, we need to talk."

She pulled out a chair opposite from him across the polished oak table. On the way down, she said, "So you plan to move out."

"I want to talk about the drowning machine."

She frowned.

"Don't play dumb. I've seen you do it."

"I don't–"

"That's why I was there that morning, when they attacked."

The crease between her glittering eyes deepened. Her chin wrinkled, her thin lips pressed together, the pale pink turning white. Then her cheeks drooped, she closed her eyes, and she exhaled. "What do you want? Free rent … I don't have much money."

He stammered, mumbled, "No, no."

She reared up, her eyes flashing again. "Then why bring it up? It's none of your business!"

"They're not through with you! I'm trying to warn you!"

A blank look began to rise through her anger. He'd seen that look before, that willfully ignorant look. He said, "I know the truth."

She lowered her head, stared at the tabletop. "So somebody told you how Mister Reeves died. Congratulations, you're quite a detective. I … I know it's insane, but I can't help myself."

"Squirrels killed him."

She nodded.

"Giant squirrels. Like the ones that attacked us."

135

She peered up at him, the blaze returning to her narrow eyes. "I've smelled reefer on your breath, Mister Donaldson. I know you eat those pain killers like candy."

"We both know dogs didn't attack us."

"Whoever told you that giant squirrels killed my husband is a liar."

"You just said–"

"Squirrels!" She thumped the table with her bony fist. He jumped, sloshing his coffee in his mug. She said, "Regular, everyday squirrels. He was helping Mister Olafson repair the roof of his barn when a squirrel startled him and he fell off the ladder and broke his neck. Mister Olafson never said anything about giant squirrels."

"So you built the machine …"

She studied him, then said, "I did. What of it?"

He sipped his coffee, which only made the taste in his mouth worse. She was obviously unstable. He began to fear that if he convinced her, she'd only become further unhinged, but it was too late to back out now. "You know that's why they attacked you."

In a frosty tone, she said, "*Fine*. Between you and me, bigger than average squirrels, not dogs, attacked me. Some kind of pack mentality, protecting their own. But I'm telling you right now, I shall never speak of this to another soul. There, are you happy?"

"No. I'm not. It wasn't pack mentality. It was the Hellers."

He caressed a blister on his right palm with his left index fingertip. Her cackles began quiet, then grew shrill. "I see. The Hellers have bred and trained attack squirrels! That's rich. And why, pray tell, would those filthy boys want to harm me?"

He clasped his hands, ignoring the blisters. "The Hellers don't breed giant squirrels. They are the giant squirrels."

Her eyes darted back and forth, both lasering on one of his eyes, then the other, and back again. She said, "Preposterous."

He couldn't think straight. The whole sordid mess, the pot dealing, the statutory rape, the murders, teetered on the tip of his tongue, then he blurted, "No, wait! Remember what you told me about the squirrel hunts, and your grandfather? If the Hellers were around back then, they must've taken revenge for that too."

She sat back, her scowl transforming to slackened shock. "Oh my Lord."

He leaned over the table. "What? What is it?"

"That's why I must have thought about dogs in the first place." Her eyes focused on him. "My Great Uncle Parker. Old Ma Heller, she cursed the squirrel hunters, claiming that they shot her son, but nobody would fess up to it, then a month or so later, dogs, they said, tore apart Uncle Parker."

"See! The hunters must've shot one of the Hellers ... I know this sounds crazy, but they must've shot one of the Hellers when he was in squirrel form. Then they waited a little while, and they got their revenge. And I'm telling you, they mean to finish the job on you, Mike Heller said so."

"My Lord." She cupped her cheeks. "How's such a thing possible on God's green earth?"

"So you believe me?"

"I ... it makes too much sense."

"They're after me too. I'm getting out of town, tonight, or tomorrow, soon as I can. I just had to warn you."

She removed her palms from her cheeks, and she gave him a hard look. He suspected she was about to curse him for being a coward. She said, "I want to show you something."

She led him to the garage. The brown Cadillac dominated one half, a work bench, with tools mounted on the pegboard on the wall above, took up the other half. The lawn mower was parked against the back wall next to a huge, locked cabinet.

She unlocked the cabinet. A chainsaw and assorted power tools perched on the shelves of the upper half. There were no shelves on the lower half. A footlocker sat on the floor of the cabinet. A big padlock sealed the footlocker. She unlocked it, and swung its lid open.

A shotgun and a rifle equipped with a scope lied in black foam padding in the bottom of the footlocker. Strapped to the inside of the lid, also on a bed of foam padding, were a matching set of revolvers, an automatic pistol, and the biggest handgun He'd ever seen. Mrs. Reeves pointed at that big gun. "That's a Magnum, just like Dirty Harry."

He was no expert on guns, so he took her word for it. He spotted boxes of shells tucked between the cabinet and the footlocker's side-wall.

"Mister Reeves was something of a firearms enthusiast," she said.

"Do they all work?"

"I maintain them. Regular cleaning and oiling, and I go out to the range and fire them once or twice a month."

"I'll be damned."

She unstrapped the Magnum. She loaded it, then handed it to him. She locked everything up tight, then took the heavy gun back. She marched into the house. He followed her. When they reached the back porch, he said, "What are you gonna do?"

She stepped outside and gripped the gun in both hands.

He scanned the backyard. No sign of squirrels, but that didn't mean they weren't watching from the shadows of the Weeds. He whispered, "They don't know that you know!"

She brandished the Magnum, hollering, "Come on then, you filthy beasts!"

He cringed. He was about to grab her and shake some sense into her, but the sight of that huge gun stopped him. Now Mike would know that he told, now Mike would probably send the whole damned pack after him.

Chapter Twenty-six

Larry looked up as the pub's front door opened. Margaret walked in with two minutes to spare before her shift officially began. Cutting it close was her new routine. He knew that she was minimizing the time she had to spend around him. She didn't look at him, another feature of her new routine.

Something about her was off. He scrutinized her approach. She moved a little stiff, but that wasn't it, no, her regulars, instead of the usual smiles and laughter, knitted their brows and asked questions in hushed voices. She hurried through them, nodding and flashing a weak smile, then flitted behind the bar and into the backroom.

He edged over to the backroom's doorway and leaned against its frame, so he could keep one eye on the bar. He looked at the back of her head while she placed her purse in her locker. He said, "I need to talk to you."

Her back stiffened. She stood still.

"Please," he said.

She turned around and looked straight at him for the first time since that morning drive home from the Hellers' party. He read nothing in her vacant expression. He squinted. He hadn't seen it at first in the backroom's gloom, but underneath a thick layer of makeup, a faint dark semi-circle traced the bottom of her left eye's socket. Having discovered the concealed shiner, he detected the puffiness around the rest of her left eye. "Oh my God ... what happened to you?"

She looked away. He took a step towards her. "Who did this to you?"

She brushed past him and left the backroom. He knew who.

He robotted through the rest of his shift-closing duties. She continued to ignore him. He retrieved his duffel bag from the backroom, then stood next to her register. When she came to ring up a sale, he still hadn't thought of the right thing to say, the implications of her bruise destroying his planned farewell speech.

Avoiding eye contact, she murmured, "Please get out of my way."

She drifted off while searching for a drink order. He stepped out from behind the bar and retreated to a shadowy spot along the wall. A few of her more dedicated regulars, a few of the more perceptive ones who'd deduced over Cheese Days that something had been brewing between him and Margaret, shot him the evil glares, as if they believed he'd blackened her eye. Meanwhile, she swiveled her head continuously, like all decent bartenders, seeking customers waiting for service. She scanned all directions except his, an oversight that he knew was proof that she was hyperaware of his presence. He also knew that he was bothering the hell out of her.

Whenever she didn't have an immediate drink order to fill, she trended toward the side of the bar opposite to him. She could've gotten that black eye in any number of ways. But there was only one obvious explanation.

He adjusted his duffel bag. He lit a cigarette. He'd made just enough in tips for a pack of smokes and a bus ticket home. He took a drag and watched her hustle. He guessed that the sooner he was gone the happier she would be. She could get back to the way things were before he showed up and ruined everything. Better for everybody if he waited out the interim at the bus stop. He took one last look, then walked out of the bar.

The beat-up blue LTD was parked in the spot directly in front of the pub. All four of the sedan's doors swung open as the pub's door banged shut behind him. Jackie got out of the front driver's side, Jay-Jay the front passenger's, and Slappy and Looey behind them. Jackie led the gang of stunted thugs toward Larry. They'd all tied their long, dirty brown hair back in sloppy ponytails. They all wore jeans except Jackie, whose baggy blue-and-green tartan-patterned shorts flapped past his kneecaps. A sleeveless jean-jacket, which Larry thought used to belong to Casey, covered Jackie's gristle-and-bone torso, the jacket's hem hanging past Jackie's hips. Jay-Jay backed his twin, Looey limped at the rear of the pack. The flinty look in Slappy's eyes assured Larry that he had no allies here.

They crowded him. Their collective unwashed musk rankled his nose, invaded his mouth. They glared at him. He shook, his field of vision blackening around the edges, shrinking to them.

"We need to talk to you," Jackie said. "Let's take a ride."

He dropped his duffel and shoved Jackie, who bashed backwards into Jay-Jay and Slappy, the twins smacking down to the pavement in a tangle of limbs, Slappy stutter-stepping to the side, and Looey back-peddling out of the way.

Larry loomed over the floundering twins and snarled, "Which one of you did it?"

Jay-Jay disentangled himself and Slappy helped him up. Jackie held his palms out towards Larry and said, "Barney did it! His idea!"

Larry thought about booting the creep in the face. Jackie scrabbled backwards and up to his feet, wisps of dirty brown hair pulled free from his ponytail. Larry said, "What do you want?"

"Tonight," Jackie said, "Midnight, you and Barney in the quarry."

Larry's gaze swept over them, stopped on Slappy, and he said, "I can't believe you're going along with this crap. Hitting a girl!"

Slappy flinched and looked down at the pavement.

"You don't show," Jackie said, "and he'll do worse things to your girl."

Fury careened up Larry's backbone. He began to tremble.

"Mike knows you told that old cunt," Jackie said. "He said you better not tell anybody else, and you better show up tonight."

Larry scowled at the weird-eyed bastard. "Where's this quarry?"

Jackie flicked a folded up sheet of notebook paper at Larry, who caught it and unfolded the handwritten directions. He studied the note, then said, "How am I supposed to get out there after what you did to my car?"

Jackie, already retreating towards the LTD, said, "That's your problem."

Larry watched them drive away, only then noticing the dispersal of the dozen or so rubberneckers. He picked up his duffel bag and started walking. He needed a drink.

Chapter Twenty-seven

Larry nursed a bottle of High Life in the last booth. He sat with his back against the wall so he could see both the neon Blatz clock mounted above the bar and the entrance to Mayslacks', a combination cheese shop and tavern on the side of the square opposite to Bub's. The minute hand on the Blatz clock clunked forward a notch, indicating ten-thirty on the dot. After adjusting for bartime, Larry calculated forty-five minutes to go before the bus would pull out of the convenience store parking lot, a block north of the square.

Larry lit another cigarette. He'd never stepped foot in Mayslacks' before. A well-lit shop, complete with aisles and a checkout counter, served as the front end. The shop featured a wide selection of cheeses, as well as sausages and specialty chocolates. The back end was a muted and darkened watering hole. The radio played low country-and-western. Four middle-aged men sat at the tiny bar, sipping beers and munching pretzels, chatting up the bartender, a short blonde whom Larry believed he'd met at that pre-Cheese Days party about a million years ago. The three booths in front of his were empty.

The bell over the shop's door tinkled. Mike and Bill stepped inside. Larry sat up straight. They ambled towards him. He glanced at the other customers. They were already turning away, muttering. Bill's hair flowed loose past his shoulders, his tinted glasses and his full, shaggy beard vibing groovy. He wore a black AC/DC tee shirt, blue jeans, and brown work boots. Mike's hair dangled above his shoulders, but his neatly-lined bangs, his clean-shaven face, his loose blue polo shirt, gray jeans, and squeaky-clean white-leather high-tops, made him seem almost preppy.

They sat down on opposite side of his booth, with Bill sliding against the wall. Bill said, "I really thought you'd stick it out for her sake."

"You keep testing us," Mike said. He sat back. "We're not unreasonable. We're rooting for you, man, against our own blood."

"It'll be a fair fight," Bill said. "Just you and him. We'll see to it that the rest of the boys are nowhere near the quarry."

Mike leaned forward, placed his elbows on the table, and looked Larry in the eyes. "Listen, we don't wanna sit here and make threats like if you don't do this, we'll kill everybody you love, your parents, your grandparents, your brothers and sisters, your nieces and nephews, everybody you care about."

"But you can't hide from us," Bill said.

"Remember what I told you?" Mike asked. "We got eyes everywhere. We speak a special language. We will find you."

"We'll know as soon as you set foot on that bus," Bill said.

Mike whispered, "Just kill the fucker. You got more than enough reason now."

"Afterwards," Bill said, "we'll pick up where we left off. Maybe get into some stronger stuff. Let's get back into the business of making money."

Larry scoffed. "What am I supposed to buy it with? You stole all my money, and you still owe me for last time."

"You handle Barney, I'll pay you what I owe," Bill said. "The rest I don't know about. Jackie and Jay-Jay brought your car back, so you'll have to talk to them. Worse comes to worse, I'm sure your connection will front you a decent quantity."

"Let's lay all the cards on the table," Mike said. "We can't stop you from walking up the block and getting on that bus. Maybe you think we're bluffing. But think about this. I happen to know that Margaret walked to work tonight. She'll be walking home, too. You get on that bus ... Barney's all revved up for a death match. You don't show, he's gotta spend all that bad energy somewhere. I won't help him, but I won't stop him from rounding up Jackie and them, and ... I don't think I have to spell it out for you."

Bill spread his hands. "But it don't have to be that way. Just go on out and face Barney. At least you'll have a fighting chance."

Mike leaned back. "And if you don't make it, you have my word they won't touch her." Mike glanced at Bill, who shrugged. Mike looked at Larry and said, "I guess we said what we came to say."

Bill nodded. "There's still time to do the right thing, man."

Mike cocked his head and raised an eyebrow. "Be a man, Larry."

Larry glanced at the Blatz clock. He sprang out of the booth, duffel bag in hand, and darted towards the door. Behind him Mike said, "Attaboy."

Chapter Twenty-eight

The handlebars wrenched sideways, this time the front tire skidding almost perpendicular, forcing Larry to shift his feet from the pedals to road. He bridged off the seat and held the ancient Schwinn up. The duffel bag slapped against his back, the weight of the Magnum punching a grunt out of him.

He stood there, the granny-bike listing underneath him, and caught his breath. His muscles blazed. His arms and shoulders kept going numb from leaning on the handlebars to support his torso. When he straightened up for relief, lactic acid seared his thighs and calves.

He wiped the sweat from his brow. The creaky three-speed sucked on gravel, the deep patches slewing the skinny tires sideways, forcing him to ride the brakes on the downslopes, a precaution against wipeouts that cost him precious momentum for the upslopes, the slow, grueling climbs sapping even more of his dwindling energy.

A rippling through the corn suggested hidden stalkers. He righted the bike and resumed pedaling. When he crested the next hill he spotted the stand of trees that landmarked the quarry's service road.

He coasted down to the entrance, lowering his feet from the pedals and letting his soles scuff along the gravel. Clumps of grass grew across the dump truck-wide dirt road. A metal post stood on each side of the entrance, its gate long gone.

He ditched the bike and pulled the Magnum from the duffel bag. He shoved a handful of extra shells in the pocket of his jeans, just in case, and then wrapped the duffel bag around the Schwinn's seat.

He took a few ginger steps before the pain abated, his toes still blistery from the day's shift and last night's cross-country escape. Full-grown trees lined both sides of the service road, the dense leafage blocking out most of the moonlight. He held the Magnum at his side, his gun arm loose and ready. If they were gonna ambush him, he figured it would be here.

He pricked up his ears. Nearby, the soft brush of leaves, the chirping chorus of crickets. Far off, a truck barreling down the highway. Nothing in-between. The night sounds held steady all the way to the end of the rutted road, and he stepped back into unobstructed moonlight as he entered the quarry proper.

On his immediate left sat a small, rickety shack, its windows busted out. On his right the quarry floor ran flat into a cornfield. Beyond the shack, a hillside loomed, its pocked and gouged wall rising at least six stories high. Larry rounded the shack, giving the potential hideout a wide berth, and he faced the labyrinth of man-sized stones scattered under the shadow of the hill.

Holding the Magnum tight against the side of his thigh, he turned in a slow circle. On the left, they could watch from the ridge above, and they could hide behind the stones below. On the right, the corn. There'd been no need to ambush him on the dark service road. In the quarry, they could surround him.

He sidled towards the corn. He decided that by now they must know that he was here. He called out, "Here I am." A slight echo returned from the quarry wall. He continued towards the corn. At least on this side they couldn't drop rocks on his head.

Barney strode out from behind a nearby stone. "I heard you tried to run away."

Larry squared himself with Barney, who, for once, was not wearing his mirrored shades. Larry kept his ears pricked for any sounds of a sneak attack from the corn.

Barney snaked his way out of the stones and stopped. He stood with his right hand behind his back. Larry judged that about twenty yards separated them. Barney said, "I'm surprised you showed up at all."

Larry recalled Margaret's blackened eye. Stiff-jawed, he said, "You shouldn't have done that to her."

"Margaret? Shucks, I didn't hardly do nothin'. Wasn't even my idea."

Larry didn't give a damn whose idea it was. "What do you got behind your back?"

"I think you know. Not as big a one as you got by your side, but I bet I can whip mine around before you can lift that cannon."

The Magnum felt like it was pulling his shoulder out of its socket. Tiny, involuntary spasms wracked his deltoid, which last night's gravedigging had reduced to jelly. Maybe Barney was right. He tried to hike the gun onto his leg, to take some of its weight on his thigh. "If I hadn't brought a gun, you would have just shot me, wouldn't you?"

Barney, a hint of a grin on his face, said, "I knew you were a prick the first time I laid eyes on you."

Larry tried not to let Barney's weird eye distract him. He felt his heartbeat slowing. He took a slow, soundless breath through his nose. He watched for Barney to twitch, for Barney to make the first move. Barney's good eye narrowed to a slit, his bug eye remained dead and wide. *Fuck this.* Larry hoisted his right arm.

The Magnum, as heavy as an anvil, resisted. Barney slung his arm from behind his back. The muscles in Larry's forearm cramped. He took a backward step with his left foot. The burst of Barney's first shot startled Larry into squeezing his own trigger while he was still hauling up the Magnum. The blast added violent propulsion to Larry's motion, and his arm jumped, jolting his shoulder, the surge ending with his gun hand high overhead.

A slug whizzed near his ear. He yanked the Magnum down and leveled it toward the sound of muffled gunfire. He fired blind, the gun kicking his arm up again. He realized he was standing still, a stationary target, and he dropped to the dirt. He slapped his left hand to the Magnum to steady it, and squeezed off two thunderous shots, waiting for the first kick to spend itself before re-sighting. He aimed at the center of the small cloud of scared up dust.

He squinted and waited for the dust to settle. Over the ringing in his ears, he heard a distant, sluggish gurgle. The dust cleared. Barney lied sprawled on his back, his chest heaving.

Larry lunged to his feet. He pointed the Magnum at Barney while shifting his head from side to side. Nobody was charging out of the corn, nobody was rushing from the stone labyrinth. He scuttled over to Barney.

The stubby handgun lied near Barney's lolling head. Larry used the instep of his boot to graze the gun along the dirt and out of Barney's reach. Barney ejected a thick cough. With his blood-slicked left hand he pawed at his ragged and gory throat. His right hand pressed down on his lower belly, his fingers dark and shiny, a septic stench wafting up to Larry's nostrils. Barney's left foot began to shudder.

Larry backed away. He looked up to the ridge and shouted, "He brought a gun too!" He took two more backwards steps toward the service road, then said, "It was a fair fight!"

He whirled and ran as fast down the service road as his injured body would allow. He sensed that his deafened ears were on the verge of popping. He couldn't hear them, but could picture them running through the trees on both sides of the road, shadowing him, giant furry bodies slipping quietly through the underbrush.

He stopped at the end of the service road and reloaded the Magnum. Its barrel warmed his fingers. He looked up and down the gravel road. No headlights in sight. He caught his breath, then went for the bike.

He unzipped the duffel bag, then thought better of stowing the gun. He zipped up the duffel bag and slung it over his shoulder. Headlights crested a hill down the road. He ducked and flattened himself against the ditch's bank. He slithered a few inches upward and propped arms against the grassy bank, aiming the Magnum at the oncoming vehicle.

The car slowed. By the way it rode low and rocked on its suspension, he recognized the Cadillac. He scrambled out of the ditch waving his arms. The Caddy stopped, and he jumped in.

Mrs. Reeves, her eyes tiny and hard, took off as soon as Larry closed his door.

"I wasn't sure if you got my message," he said.

"Did you get him? I heard shots."

"I got him."

"One down, then."

Larry stared at the huge gun in his hand. "Maybe we should head back home, regroup, think this out. I mean, I did what they wanted me to do. There's no rush now."

"No. They won't be expecting it. Now's the perfect time."

Chapter Twenty-eight

Larry shifted from a crouch to sitting directly on the soil. He arched his back, trying to make it crack. He glanced at Reeves. Her agility had surprised him, as she veered through the corn without disturbing the stalks, her coarse green shirt and khakis blending with the sun-bleached leafage. She kneeled and watched the Heller place, as patient as any seasoned hunter squatting in a duck blind. She cradled the shotgun. The automatic was in the holster strapped to her hip. He wore the revolvers in twin holsters and gripped the rifle. After his struggles with the Magnum, he had decided to leave it in the duffel bag.

They spied on the Hellers from four rows deep in the field. They could see the backyard, and the porch door, and the LTD, an International Harvester that was without wheels and up on blocks, and the camper. All three vehicles were parked underneath the bare branches of the huge, dead oak.

The camper seemed to have rolled in a long time ago. Hellers had streamed out of it, some carrying Barney's corpse toward the barns, others going into the house and turning on every light so that all the windows glowed bright. The Heller boys kept coming and going between the barns and the house. But Larry knew it couldn't have been that long, because somebody had cranked Dio's *Holy Diver* album soon after the camper arrived, and side two hadn't played through yet.

His guts churned. Yeah, he'd killed two men now, but both in self-defense. This was something else entirely. He kept trying to talk her out of it, that this wasn't the plan, but she kept shushing him. He was about to give it another try when Mike, Bill, and Jackie, arguing, already slurring, emerged from the barn complex while passing a bottle of Jack amongst themselves. The moonlight showed the dirt streaks on their jeans and tee-shirts, and on Jackie's bare chest. They stopped near the oak and passed the bottle, their voices carrying over Dio's leather-lunged, sword-and-sorcery metal to Larry and Reeves' position in the corn.

"I got cause!" Jackie said, thrust his chest out. "I got fuckin' cause!"

"Nobody's sayin' you don't," Mike said.

"All we're sayin' is you gotta hold off until we get his connection," Bill said. "Then you can do any fuckin' thing you want."

Mike took a swig of whiskey, then said, "As long as it's quiet. Things been too loud lately. Too loud man, too loud. We gotta settle things down, for a while, anyways."

Bill took the bottle and jabbed it towards Jackie while saying, "Yeah! Anyways, right now, we gotta pay homage."

"Damned straight," Jackie said. "But I want your fuckin' word."

Mike traced a cross over his heart. Jackie nodded, and they weaved around the oak and into the house.

Reeves turned to Larry and hissed, "What were they talking about?"

"I'll explain it later." He gazed at the house. Nothing they said shocked him, that they'd eventually demand to meet his supplier, that Jackie would be the next one to come after him. "They're probably gonna go pretty late. Are you sure you wanna wait till they pass out?"

"The longer they carry on the easier they'll be to deal with." She began to creep down the row. "C'mon." She stopped when they could see into the living room window. They watched the Hellers shotgun beers, guzzle whiskey, and smoke pot.

The Hellers partied through Black Sabbath's *Heaven and Hell*, then Accept's *Balls to the Wall*, both in their entirety. They made it through side one of Iron Maiden's *Piece of Mind*, and part of the flip side, when someone abruptly turned off the music, startling Larry out of his stupor.

Mrs. Reeves watched the house like a hawk as the lights winked out room by room. She whispered, "I think I have a better idea."

Larry experienced a wave of relief. He began to rise, anticipating that she would throw in the towel for the night.

She said, "We'll burn their house down."

He froze in a half-crouch. He stammered.

"That old place will go up like a tinderbox," she said. "The police will think that one of them fell asleep with a cigarette in his mouth." She stood up, her knees crackling.

"Where are you going?" He asked.

"They must have gasoline in one of the barns." She handed him the shotgun. "Here, hold this." She drew the automatic and started up the row toward the barns.

He quaked with the urge to scream at her as she slipped into the shadows of the outbuildings. A rusty screech sounded from the barns, making his jaw clench. Moments later Reeves hurried out from the barns, lugging a two-gallon gas can in her left hand, holding the automatic ready in her right. She made a beeline for the house.

"Who's there?"

Before he could pivot towards the porch door, he recognized Meryl's voice. Meryl peered towards the barns. Reeves ducked behind the dead oak. Meryl stared right at the tree. Reeves wasn't fooling her for a second. Meryl said, "I can see you."

Reeves stepped out from behind the tree. She pointed the automatic at Meryl. The way she straightened her elbow, the way she leaned forward a little, Larry could tell that she meant to pull the trigger.

Larry dropped the shotgun and rifle. He drew the revolvers. He heard a shot. He fired at Reeves. And again. And again, till both revolvers clicked empty. Reeves was down. Meryl was hunched down, her right hand touching the ground for balance. She seemed unhurt. Sirens whooped and red lights flashed.

Chapter Thirty-four

Larry sat on the cold steel bench and stared at the gray concrete floor. He took shallow breaths. After three months he still wasn't used to that ever-present, sickly-sweet stench, like backed-up sewers after a heavy rain.

He looked up at the gray walls of the holding cell. He figured it was his mother. His father hadn't come in a month. The old man finally realized that Larry was not going to explain himself. But Larry knew that he was still in mom's prayers, because she told him so. She kept him up to date on things, like how adorable Deanne's baby was, and how healthy and spunky the little tyke was. She kept chipping away at him, she kept probing, kept searching for a nerve, but he would never tell her a thing.

The door opened, and the guard stuck his head inside. "Donaldson! Let's go!" Larry shuffled through the door and into the visiting area. The guard pointed down the row of booths. "Number Six."

Larry took his time. She made him take this long walk along the other booths at least once a week. He was in no hurry to face those tearful eyes. He glanced at the booths as he passed by. They were more like cubicles, with partitions separating each one, the cloth-covered walls rising to the ceiling. A white counter and a thick pane of glass divided the con side from the civilian side. Each side had a pair of hard plastic chairs bolted to the floor. Phones were affixed to each side of the counter. The mouthpieces always stank of stale cigarettes.

He rounded Booth Number Six, expecting to see mom's anxious smile. On the other side of the glass, Mike's easy smile awaited him. Mike wore a white dress shirt and a black tie. His hair was slicked back, his face shaved smooth. He looked like he was on his way to church. Or court. He was sitting, the phone already in his hand.

Larry realized that he was gawking. He sat down and picked up the phone.

"How's the big house treating you?" Mike asked. "Joliet, damn! I guess they don't stick convicted murderers in county lockup, do they? Don't drop the soap!"

"What do you want?"

"Hey, chill out man, this is a friendly visit. I would've been out sooner, but I had to wait for the heat to die down."

Larry mashed his lips together. He knew why Mike was here. Mike was afraid that three months in prison might break Larry. Mike was here to deliver a warning.

"You didn't say much at your trial," Mike said.

Larry ground his teeth. He didn't say anything at his trial. Not to anyone. His lack of cooperation with the DA had gotten him a life sentence for the murder of Mrs. Reeves. Nobody knew what he and Reeves had been doing out there, armed to the teeth. Nobody but the Hellers, and Officer Jim. And maybe even the Hellers didn't know why Larry had shot Mrs. Reeves dead. The moment the cops had slapped the cuffs on him, and he had looked from Reeves' dead body to all the bleary-eyed Hellers blinking back at him, was the moment he'd decided that jail was the only safe place for him.

"Just what exactly were you gonna do that night," Mike said, "if the cops weren't there?"

Larry snorted. His lawyer, the public defender, had told him how it had gone down that night. Some folks had called the cops about the gunshots in the quarry. The cops figured that it was just the Hellers. It wouldn't be the first time that the boys had gotten shitfaced and had gone shooting. The cops had decided to give the boys time to drink themselves silly and, when the boys were sure to be passed out, the cops had planned to swoop in and disarm them. Maybe catch Slappy while they were at it. They'd been rolling up to the lane, their headlights off, when they had heard Larry's gunfire. Since then, Larry had killed a lot of time wondering whether or not he would have tried to commit suicide by cop, if he hadn't emptied both revolvers.

He leveled a cool gaze at Mike and said, "You got nothing to worry about." He shrugged. "Who'd believe me?"

Mike raised and eyebrow. "Wow, you really got your yard-stare down. That's good. I guess I don't have to tell ya what'll happen to Margaret if you go tellin' tales out of school. But just in

153

case you don't give a fuck about her any more, you got another reason to keep your mouth shut."

Larry almost smiled. he supposed this was where Mike would claim to have friends on the inside, friends who could get to Larry any time Mike wanted.

Mike said, "Meryl's pregnant."

Larry scrutinized Mike's face, hunting for the lie.

"That's right," Mike said. "I hear you weren't much for protection." He beamed. "She's gonna keep it! So, congratulations!"

Larry knew it was true. It couldn't tickle Mike so much if it wasn't true.

Mike waggled his index finger at Larry while saying, "But before you go handing out cigars, you might wanna wait till she pops. Ya see, if the kid has a tail, then it's probably mine."

Mike winked at Larry. He hung up the phone and left.

THE END

www.ingramcontent.com/pod-product-compliance
Lightning Source LLC
Chambersburg PA
CBHW070931130626
46555CB00001B/387